Deceptive Promises

Amber Miller

Heartsong Presents

As always, my appreciation goes out to my loving husband and the rest of my family on both sides. I also want to thank my critique group in the Springs who helped me whip this book into shape. Thank you also to my editor, JoAnne Simmons, and my content editors, Becky Fish and Rachel Overton. I'd be lost without you both! Top gratitude goes to God, my heavenly Father, for instilling the love and joy of writing. It's a blessing to be able to use these gifts to touch others.

A note from the Author:
I love to hear from my readers! You may correspond with me by writing:

Amber Miller
Author Relations
PO Box 721
Uhrichsville, OH 44683

ISBN 978-1-60260-189-5

DECEPTIVE PROMISES

All scripture quotations are taken from the King James Version of the Bible.

All of the characters and events in this book are fictitious. Any resemblance to actual persons, living or dead, or to actual events is purely coincidental.

Our mission is to publish and distribute inspirational products offering exceptional value and biblical encouragement to the masses.

PRINTED IN THE U.S.A.

Miss Scott, I wish that I could tell you everything about what I do, why I am here, and my mission."

He looked away and saw several boats traveling upriver. "But I cannot."

Margret placed a hand on his arm, and he relished the comfort the gesture offered. "Mr. Lowe, I understand the need to keep certain things confidential. And I promise not to press you for more than you are able to share. Should my curiosity get the better of me, I will not take offense if you must avoid answering my questions."

Samuel couldn't find the words to form a reply. He looked down at her open and trusting expression, encouraged by how easily she agreed to take him at his word. Breezes from the river blew around them and stirred the loose tendrils of hair at the nape of her neck. The lace edge of her lappet cap fluttered as well. She had changed so much since he last saw her—mature and more aware of the importance of the events taking place around her. But she was still young. He had to remain mindful of that fact.

He bent at the waist slightly and held the fingertips of one of her hands between his thumb and fingers as he captured her gaze. "Miss Scott, I cannot tell you how happy I am to hear you make that promise. And in return, I shall make a promise of my own. In due time, I promise to tell you everything about my duties. For now, despite what you may learn or hear about me, I must ask that you trust your heart before forming any conclusions."

He brushed the pads of his thumbs across her knuckles and inwardly thrilled when she shivered. Whether from his touch or the cool breeze, Samuel couldn't say for certain, but in his mind, it was the former.

AMBER MILLER is a freelance Web designer and author whose articles and short stories have appeared in local, national, and international publications. Her writing career began as a columnist for her high school and college newspapers. Her first publication in a book appeared in the form of nine contributions (as a single!) to *101 Ways to Romance Your Marriage* by Debra White Smith. She is a member of American Christian Fiction Writers and Historical Romance Writers. Some of her hobbies include traveling, music, movies, and interacting with other writers. At age three, she learned to read and hasn't put down books since. Recently married, she lives with her husband and fellow writer, Stuart, in beautiful Colorado Springs. Visit her Web site to learn more or to contact her: www.ambermiller.com.

Books by Amber Miller

HEARTSONG PRESENTS
HP784—Promises, Promises
HP803—Quills & Promises

one

Strattford House, near New Castle,
(the northernmost of Pennsylvania's three lower counties)
Christina and Brandywine River Valley, late August 1774

Margret Scott started to hoist her petticoats, but decorum made her pause. She stood at the tree canopy marking the entrance to her family's farm. Paying heed to the presence of the servants and fieldworkers, she started at a brisk walk down the lane toward the main house. As her home came into view, her speed increased. A moment later, mindful of her appearance, she resumed walking. Alternating between almost running and maintaining a ladylike pace, she finally reached the front porch. This was the most exciting news she'd heard in all of her fourteen years.

"Mama!"

She burst through the front door, cringing when it slammed against the block of wood in the corner of the entryway. Mama would scold her for that one.

"Margret Scott!" Mama's voice preceded her appearance from the kitchen into the main hallway. Elanna Hanssen Scott was a kind and generous woman, but she did not tolerate ill manners.

"Sorry, Mama." Margret tucked her chin against her chest. She fought hard to catch her breath as she peered up at Mama and offered an apologetic smile.

A grin tugged at Mama's lips. "Child, what am I to do with you? You do try one's patience." She sighed. "Now, what is so important that you could not enter our house in a more subdued manner?"

Margret inhaled a sharp breath. "Oh, Mama! You will never believe it. You know that Papa and I were visiting at the Hanssen farm." At Mama's nod, Margret continued. "And I am quite excited!"

Mama wiped her hands on her apron and quirked one eyebrow. "Are you going to tell me, or shall I have to wait until the news arrives from town?"

"There is a special meeting about delegates being sent from New Castle to Philadelphia. Grandfather spoke of a private meeting with the assembly that is being held in secret." Margret flung out her arms and spun in a circle, then she clasped her hands together just below her chin. "The mere idea is simply breathtaking! They mentioned something about a congress and how every colony except Georgia is sending representatives. I do not know much more, but delegates from our very own assembly have been invited. Oh, how I wish Papa or Uncle Edric was going. They could write to us of everything they see. Just imagine! Philadelphia. It is such a big city. They no doubt have the latest fashions and goods. What happens there is quite important. And men from right here in New Castle will be there with other delegates."

"Margret, dear, will you take a moment to breathe?"

Margret paused and stared. Had she really just rambled without pausing for air? It was a wonder she *didn't* swoon. She started to calm, but the amusement on Mama's face roused Margret's excitement again. A grin graced her lips. "And I have yet to tell you the best part."

"Pray, do tell me soon, my daughter, before you burst the linen in your stays."

Margret grabbed hold of Mama's flour-covered hands and squeezed. "Grandfather has persuaded Papa to allow me to accompany them into town, provided you come as well. Papa said a ship recently arrived in port, teeming with crates and barrels of all shapes and sizes. Can you imagine it? There will be so many people about, and the shops will no doubt be open to everyone. We can see the latest fashions and styles and perhaps even purchase a new bonnet."

"A recent shipment of goods, you say?" Mama withdrew one hand from Margret's clasp and reached up to touch her hair. "I suppose I should make myself a bit more presentable for a town visit to purchase a few necessities." A twinkle entered her eyes as she looked down at Margret. "We cannot have the family of assembly members appearing less than fashionable, now can we?"

"Oh, Mama, you can be quite silly sometimes."

"No more so than you, my dear." Mama traced her finger down Margret's face and tapped her on the nose. "Now, off with you. I am certain the men will not be far behind, so you should not tarry any longer with me."

Margret threw her arms around Mama, then she stepped back and pressed her hands down the front of her petticoats to smooth out the wrinkles. She winked, assumed a proper stance, and tamed her expression into one of polite indifference. "I promise to present myself in the most genteel of manners. My decorum will be impeccable."

Mama chuckled. "At least until you once again get caught up in the excitement of the moment."

Although she tried hard, Margret couldn't tame her expression. The smile pulling at her mouth finally won out, and she turned toward the stairs. Mama shook her head and disappeared again in the direction of the kitchen.

❧

"Nicholas, come help your grandfather, please."

Papa's voice sounded from the other side of the carriage

where he extended a hand to Mama. A moment later, Margret's younger brother Nicholas skidded around the side and assisted Papa in helping Grandfather Gustaf onto his seat. Grandmother Raelene wanted to stay home and work on her quilt, but Margret knew wagon rides weren't exactly comfortable for her. It wasn't easy seeing either of her grandparents struggle, but despite their age, they both still had a firm command of the running of the farm. And they stayed abreast of political developments. Margret didn't have as much interest in affairs of state as her parents and grandparents did, but she tried to pay attention to what was important. The results of the congress gathering in Philadelphia were sure to become the center of conversation for some time. Speculation had been high in recent months. Something would happen soon. Margret prayed they'd be ready when it did.

"Will you be joining us, young one, or do you intend to stand and stare as the carriage leaves you behind?"

Margret started at Grandfather's voice and looked up to see him smiling down at her. His expression showed he had guessed her thoughts. Leave it to Grandfather to put on a strong face for everyone. Accepting Papa's outstretched hand, Margret climbed into the carriage and took her seat. Grandfather placed an arm around her shoulders and pulled her close. Margret snuggled against him, determined to enjoy the peaceful ride into town.

Before she knew it, they approached the outskirts of New Castle. The activity level increased tenfold. Wagons rumbled along the cobblestone streets, and horse hooves clopped as they pulled carriages or held lone riders. As Papa drove the carriage into the center of town, the raucous voices of the townspeople joined the symphony of sounds that represented town life.

Margret soaked up the palpable joy and enthusiasm shared

by her fellow colonists at the latest arrival of goods. But another level of anticipation existed. Papa surreptitiously pointed out several gentlemen whose names Margret recognized from various conversations. Ladies waved lace handkerchiefs in the air. Men raised their cocked hats high. Their driver stopped the carriage to allow the throngs of people to part and allow them room to pass.

Nicholas leaned forward and tapped Margret's knee as he jerked his head to the side.

"That is the mayor of Wilmington, John McKinly."

Margret turned to see a well-dressed gentleman approach the print shop a block ahead of them. He certainly looked like a man of some importance. And the way several townsfolk stepped aside to let him pass showed they felt the same way.

"Papa and Grandfather Gustaf invited him for supper one evening a few months back." Nicholas's voice interrupted her thoughts. "He is quite influential. I remember Papa talking about his service during the war with the French a few years ago. They were both majors, even though Papa served with a British regiment while Mayor McKinly commanded the New Castle militia." He looked at Papa—whose face reflected admiration that his son knew so much—then continued with pride. "Standing next to him are the three lawyers being sent as delegates: Thomas McKean, George Read, and Caesar Rodney."

Margret straightened in her seat and squinted as she peered at the three men.

"Mama, is not Mr. McKean the man who assisted you when that journalist tried to deceive you?" That was one of Margret's favorite stories.

"Yes," Mama replied with a smile at Papa.

Margret's breath caught in her throat. Had it not been for Mr. McKean, Mama might have married the journalist and not Papa. "I wish I could have been there to see it." She placed one hand on her heart. "Can you imagine having a man come to your home to call only to have his devious plans revealed by a notable statesman and the deputy attorney general?"

Papa took Mama's hand in his and bestowed a loving smile upon his wife as the wagon moved forward again. "I owe the life I have to Mr. McKean. But had he not succeeded, I would have found another way to secure your mother's affection."

Looking back and forth between her parents, Margret prayed that one day she would be as fortunate as they in marriage.

"Father, why has this meeting been called in secret?"

Nicholas's question drew everyone's attention back to the matter at hand.

"We have grown weary of the legislature across the ocean dictating to us how and when we are able to export and import our goods." Papa cleared his throat, then he lowered his voice as two British soldiers crossed the street from the sidewalk near them. "We have protested the taxes that Britain attempted to levy upon us for stamps to mail our letters, tea to serve in our homes, and sugar to sweeten our meals. And we will continue to protest until they realize we deserve the right to make those decisions for ourselves."

"But despite everything, they have not listened," Grandfather Gustaf added. "Instead, their presence has increased, and their attempts to control us have almost become unbearable."

Papa nodded. "That is the reason for the Continental Congress meeting in Philadelphia. But *our* meeting is to give a proper send-off to the three delegates and discuss the topics that may be part of the gathering up north."

Nicholas leaned forward. "And the reason for the secret meeting is to prevent any British from knowing what is happening?"

"Yes, this is why we must do all that we can to gather unnoticed." Papa signaled the driver to halt the carriage. He turned to Mama and touched her cheek. "This is where we part, my dear. We shall leave you and Margret to your tasks and meet you two hours hence in front of the town hall."

Mama gathered a burlap satchel in her hands and three handwoven baskets as she shifted toward the carriage door. The driver opened it and extended a hand first to Mama then to Margret. When they were both standing on the cobblestone street, Mama looked up at Papa. "We shall be waiting by the steps when your meeting concludes."

The driver closed the door and resumed his seat. As he snapped the reins and set the carriage in motion once more, Margret watched Papa, Grandfather Gustaf, and Nicholas continue around the back side of the buildings to the rear of the print shop. She prayed the meeting would go well.

"Margret, dear," Mama said as she touched Margret's shoulder, "let us not tarry long. We have many things to do and only a small amount of time in which to do them."

She would never have been allowed to come to town without Mama, but Margret wanted to walk around the center of town, see the shops, and look in the windows. If she stayed with Mama the entire time, she might not have that chance.

"Mama?"

"Yes, dear?"

"Would it not help us more if we each got a few items on our own?"

Mama tilted her head and regarded Margret with a curious glance. She narrowed her eyes as if trying to determine whether Margret had an ulterior motive. A moment later, her lips twitched. "You wish to have additional time so that you might see the new items that have arrived on the shipment. Am I correct?"

Mama didn't look upset. Only amused. So Margret grinned and extended her hands in a helpless gesture. "It is why I pleaded with Papa to allow me to come."

Mama tapped Margret on the nose. "Very well. You will need to go to the candle shop, the basket weaver's, and the apothecary's." She held out the three baskets, and Margret took them. "I will be at the silversmith's when you finish. Please come find me there."

"Yes, Mama." Margret dipped into a quick curtsy, then she skipped off in the direction of the basket weaver's. If she saw to her tasks first, she would have more than enough time to visit the other shops.

A little over an hour later, she closed the door behind her after leaving the apothecary's shop, having completed her errands. As she walked down the five steps to the sidewalk, Margret shielded her eyes and glanced up at the sky. By the sun's position, she guessed she had about forty minutes before the meeting at the print shop ended. She was about five blocks from the silversmith's. When she reached an alleyway, she stopped. The other end came out near the north end of the town square. That would take her right past the main street of shops. Perfect.

Margret walked about a quarter of the way down the alley but stopped when she saw two men standing close to one another, speaking in hushed tones. It was obvious by the way one of them kept glancing over his shoulder that neither one of them wanted to get caught. As quietly as possible, she took several steps backward, praying she could escape undetected. She had almost made it when her foot kicked a tin can lying on the ground.

She froze.

The two men stopped and looked in her direction.

Time seemed to stand still as she stared at the men. They

looked at each other then again at her. She didn't know what they were thinking, but if their choice for a meeting place was any indication, the fact that she saw them couldn't be a good thing.

"I. . .I. . ." Margret swallowed against the lump in her throat, trying hard to slow the pounding of her heart. "Do excuse me. I did not mean to interrupt." She took a shallow breath. "I shall just be on my way."

One of the men said something to the other, and the second man left in the opposite direction. The one who spoke took a few steps toward her. Margret didn't know whether to continue walking backward or turn and run. Either way the man was sure to catch her. At least if she turned around, she had a better chance of avoiding him.

But as soon as she stepped out of the alley and into the street, she ran into the middle of a group of British soldiers. The sack in her hands fell to the ground.

"Well, well, what have we here?" One of the men reached out and tipped up her face with his thumb and forefinger under her chin. "And what would cause a delicate young lady such as yourself to be sneaking about in the alleyways of this town?"

"Perhaps she is returning from a meeting with a secret beau, and she does not wish her mother or father to learn of her whereabouts," another soldier suggested.

"Or she might be going to meet a beau with the same thought in mind." A third soldier snickered, but Margret couldn't see him.

The first still lightly held her chin with his fingers. She dared not move. Fear at what they might do helped her feet stay rooted to the ground. From the corner of her eye, she saw a man exit the alleyway. She caught a flash of his red coat, and her heart beat twice as fast.

Could her situation get any worse?

The soldier in front of her turned, and a smirk formed on his lips. "It appears we were both right. Only it seems as if our little lady was meeting her beau in the alley."

Margret felt, rather than saw, the other man approach. As she watched the soldier in front of her, his expression changed from one of smugness to one of concern. In a flash, the soldier dropped his arms and tucked his chin toward his chest as he took a step away from her.

"Does your commander not keep you busy enough during your visit to town that you must resort to tormenting a poor, innocent girl?"

"Our apologies, Lieutenant." The leader of the threesome doffed his hat and took another step away from Margret. "We were not aware that the two of you were acquainted."

"Whether we are or not is none of your concern. But your treatment of this young lady *is* a concern."

Margret wanted more than anything to turn and look at the man who rescued her, but instead, she studied her shoes.

"Now, I do believe you owe her an apology. And once that is done, I expect you to return to your duties."

"I am humbly sorry, miss," the first said.

"My sincerest apologies, miss," the second added.

"Do forgive us," said the third.

Without a backward glance, they scrambled off.

As Margret bent to retrieve her sack, her heel caught on the edge of her skirt, and she lost her balance. Arms flailing, she attempted to remain standing, but it was no use. As she joined her sack on the ground, a cloud of dust exploded around her.

A warm, masculine laugh sounded above her head, and she braved a glance to locate the source. Words failed her as she gazed up into the face of a young man in a British officer's uniform. No wonder the other soldiers hastened to obey him so quickly. Heat rose to her cheeks at her embarrassing position, but she couldn't take her eyes off the handsome man standing over her. A few unruly chestnut strands escaped the confines of his pigtail to blow about his shoulders as he looked down at her.

The soldier chuckled and extended his hand. "Do allow me to assist you. Then, perhaps we can exchange introductions."

Margret swallowed her pride and accepted his help. His strong grip lifted her easily, and he held on a moment longer than necessary before releasing her hand. She fought back the shiver that threatened to run up her back. Gathering her wits, she faced the soldier.

"I do appreciate your coming to my aid, sir, and preventing me from a most embarrassing situation."

The soldier bowed, never taking his gaze from her. "It was my pleasure. Now, may I introduce myself?" He straightened. "I am Samuel Lowe, recently arrived from the area of New York formerly run by the East India Trading Company."

Margret dipped into a curtsy, but the packages in her arms prevented her from using her fan to conceal her face. "Pleased to meet you, Mr. Lowe. My name is Margret Scott."

He regarded her for a moment. She wasn't certain, but she thought she saw a brief flash of recognition in his eyes. He reached for her right hand and bowed over it, his self-assured smirk making her heart race.

"The pleasure is all mine, I assure you."

☙

Samuel straightened and continued studying young Margret Scott. If his sources were correct, she was the eldest daughter of Major Madison Scott and the granddaughter of Gustaf Hanssen. But the importance of her family didn't stop there. She also had an uncle who held an esteemed position with the assembly. Perhaps more than good fortune brought her to cross his path.

"Now," he began, extending his elbow toward her as he reached for the sack she had dropped, "let us return you to whatever it is that brings you to town, and perhaps you can enlighten me about yourself as we walk."

Margret hesitated, darting a glance around her as if looking for someone or something. Samuel took that moment to peer down the alley and saw that Thomas had returned. He signaled his friend to wait for him and received a nod in return before turning his attention back to Margret. Slowly she reached her right hand out toward him but didn't quite touch him.

Samuel tucked her hand into the crook of his arm and gave it a light pat. "By my troth, I promise that no harm shall come to you."

That seemed to reassure her, but she didn't offer any verbal response, leaving it up to him to carry the conversation.

"So, how did you come to be walking about town without a companion?"

He felt her stiffen for a second, then she relaxed. "I am not alone, Mr. Lowe. I have come to town with my mother and several other members of my family to. . ." She stopped and appeared to consider her words before continuing. "To purchase some much-needed supplies."

She seemed to be withholding specific details. If Samuel's assumptions were correct, her vague response made sense. He knew of the secret meeting at the back of the print shop, but he couldn't tell her about it without giving away his true identity.

"Ah. And are you to rendezvous with your mother or someone else in your family at any specific location?" Samuel tipped his hat at a passerby, receiving nothing but a look of disdain in reply. He couldn't tell whether his uniform elicited that response or the fact that he escorted a girl several years his junior.

"Yes." Margret's voice brought his attention back to her. "I am to meet Mama at the silversmith's when I complete my purchases."

"Then to the silversmith's we shall go."

He started to cross the street, when she paused. The pressure against his arm from her hand stopped him as well.

"Mr. Lowe, would it not be faster if we were to take Second Street?" Her arm crossed in front of them both as she pointed to their right.

"Yes, of course." He recovered his intentional blunder and turned them down the adjoining street. "I have not spent much time here, so certain shortcuts are unfamiliar to me. You, no doubt, are an expert at the layout of this town."

"Yes, I journey north from our farm as often as possible. So much about life here excites me and begs me to take part. The people, the activity, the new fabrics Mrs. Thomason imports. It is far more interesting than life on our farm, although I do my best to see to my responsibilities there as well."

Just as he had hoped, Margret's curiosity turned the conversation away from him and offered him the opportunity to learn more about her.

"And is your farm located far from town?"

"No, but there is so much to do at home that we do not often have the opportunity to come. Papa works at the shipyard in Wilmington, and Uncle Edric lives here in town. I visit when I am able, but it is not as often as I would like."

If he had any doubts about her family, she had just given him reason to toss them all aside. "It might be best that you remain safely tucked away on your farm during times of unrest such as we have right now."

Margret peered up at him with an innocent expression that reminded Samuel of her youth. Although she possessed a blossoming beauty that appealed to him, it wouldn't be wise to encourage anything further at this point.

"Unrest? Do you refer to the dissatisfaction of many colonists toward the British?" She gave him an appraising glance and regarded his uniform with a mixture of apprehension and interest. "In truth, I do not know that it is safe for me to be seen in your company."

Her guarded expression said far more than any words. And the way she paid close attention to each person they passed gave credence to her doubts. Samuel needed a way to convince her that he meant no harm. But what could he do?

two

Before Margret decided to pursue the line of reasoning that might put an end to their conversation, Samuel shifted her sack in his right arm, then he covered her hand and brought them both to a halt. "I do speak of the colonists' opinions, but I beseech you not to judge me by my uniform alone. Those soldiers you encountered upon your exit from the alley"—he jerked a thumb back toward Water Street—"more closely resemble the type of British many despise."

She looked over her shoulder in the direction he pointed, then she turned her appreciative gaze on him. "And I have you to thank for coming to my rescue."

Samuel felt drawn by her unabashed adoration. To her, he no doubt played the part of knight in shining armor to perfection. And while that thought gave him a certain amount of pleasure, he couldn't allow it to go too far.

He inclined his head. "You are quite welcome, Miss Scott."

"I confess that I know only bits and pieces about all that is happening between the British and the colonists." Margret's abrupt change of subject startled him as she started them walking again. "My visits to town involve social engagements and visiting the various shops to see the new merchandise that has been imported."

"And young men, no doubt," Samuel added, winking when she looked up at him.

Her cheeks colored in an attractive manner, and she averted her gaze. A moment later, she snapped open her fan and waved it back and forth in front of her face.

Samuel chuckled, enjoying the antics of this young woman, teetering on the edge of womanhood. Yet he wondered just how truthful this young woman was being with him. Now that he had confirmed her family lineage, he wasn't fully convinced she could be as ignorant of the developments around them as she claimed.

"Be that as it may," he began, bringing the conversation around to the political topics again, "I have observed a good number of townsfolk who have been more than eager to speak out against the atrocities they claim the British are enacting."

"Yes, I have heard similar things."

"And I would rather see them proceed with caution where the British are concerned, especially in regard to the taxes Britain is imposing or their other attempts to govern the colonies here. Britain is quite a force to be reckoned with. When word reaches the government of the dissension among so many colonists in this area, it is bound to react in ways that might make the situations worse than they are right now."

"Do Britain and the governing party truly have the upper hand?"

"At the moment, yes. But should the colonists rally together, they will no doubt present a strong case against Britain's ruling decisions and gain a modicum of power. However, they will also be faced with the consequences of those actions."

Margret inhaled a sharp breath. "How serious do you believe it could become?"

Samuel regarded the young woman. She continued to walk, but puzzlement was reflected in her widened eyes and parted lips. He turned to face her again. A slight breeze stirred the caramel-colored tendrils of hair around her ears, yet he resisted the urge to tuck them back into place.

"Britain, like any ruling power, does not take rebellion lightly." He weighed his words, careful to appear to be supporting neither the colonists nor the British. "The colonists need to keep that uppermost in their minds or risk the threat of harsher reactions from across the ocean."

"But if they merely present their reasons for disagreeing with the acts of the British, why would there be a need for any reaction?"

She seemed so innocent. When her actions had first caught his attention, he had assumed her to be interested in what all young maidens her age found appealing. Young men, the latest fashions, social events in town, and the like. And from the way she spoke, Samuel knew that to be true. Now, however, his words had struck a chord in her, and her questions showed an intelligent mind wanting to be informed.

"There are people everywhere who make it a point to listen to conversations and report back the results." Samuel kept his gaze forward and observed everyone they passed along the street. At a corner ahead of them, several British soldiers clustered together, speaking to one another. Two others in the characteristic red coats were far in front, heading toward the town center. "Just because the colonists take care to present their dissatisfaction in a respectable manner," he said, returning his gaze to her, "it does not guarantee that reports of certain aspects of their feelings or the unrest will not be altered before they reach British ears."

Margret slipped the string of her fan around her wrist and allowed it to dangle as she pressed two fingers to her lips. "Would that actually happen?"

"As unfortunate as it is for the colonists, yes."

She narrowed her eyes and regarded him in silence. Samuel's heart pounded, and his breathing came in shallow spurts. He'd better be more careful. As far as he knew, she still wasn't sure who he was or why he was here. But if he was going to gain her trust, he had to give her a reason.

She shrugged. "Then I suppose they will simply have to unite together against a common foe but take care not to allow their plans to be discovered."

Samuel fought hard not to disparage her in any way. She possessed such a simplistic view of the circumstances. Then again, from the little she'd revealed, she'd no doubt grown up hearing vague reports from the assembly filtered through her father, uncle, and grandfather. It was no wonder she failed to see the true depth of all that was taking place. After all, she was just a girl. Her life remained centered on baking, cleaning, sewing, and other tasks around the family farm. On the other hand, educating her might prove to be the amusement he needed to break the monotony of his duties.

With a grin, he crossed his arms and raised one eyebrow. "And just how do you suppose they do that?"

She leaned closer to him while still maintaining a respectful distance. "As I have learned, it is quite possible for men to conceal their intentions and present an opposing front when necessary. I see no reason why the colonists would be any different."

For a split second, Samuel's breath caught. She couldn't have deduced his true purpose here, could she? Her unassuming expression assured him that was impossible. She merely answered him based upon her own experiences through her family. That didn't mean he could let down his guard, though. He had to be more careful.

"Yes, but what do you think might happen at a meeting of a select group of colonists if one of the men present should betray their confidences?"

Margret inhaled a sharp breath and covered her mouth with a gloved hand. "That would not be possible! The men involved have proven their loyalty. Otherwise, they would not have been invited to attend."

She gasped and turned to stare straight ahead, her lips pressed in a thin line. No doubt she had said more than she intended, and with that slip, she had given him insight into what she'd been told about the meeting at the print shop. It wasn't much, but it was enough for him to confirm she had overheard more than she willingly offered.

"But you yourself just said that men are capable of concealing their true intentions."

She opened her mouth to respond but closed it just as quickly, perhaps weighing her words before answering. "Be that as it may, Mr. Lowe, I cannot believe any differently than that the colonists who are at odds with Britain are honest, upstanding men whose only desire is to bring benefit to their families and the colonies they represent."

"And I am not saying that is not the case. I am merely presenting the alternative argument as a means of proving that the unexpected *can* happen."

Understanding dawned on her face. A moment later, a smile teased the corner of her lips, and a twinkle entered her eyes. "You have more than proven that today, Mr. Lowe, with your surprise rescue and continued appearance with me."

Her rapid change from uncertain to assertive caught him off guard. Was she flirting with him? Her words and actions seemed to indicate that. What other little secrets did young Margret conceal beneath her innocent facade?

Samuel tipped the corner of his hat. "As have you, my dear, with your engaging wit and impressive intellect."

Once again, a charming pink crept into her cheeks. Margret took a deep breath. "Thank you." She inclined her head slightly as a gleam entered her eyes. "But I would not have accomplished that feat had it not been for your equally impressive ability to provoke discussion."

"To that, I cannot argue." Samuel grinned and was rewarded

with a beaming smile from Margret at his boast.

"My dear sir, I—"

Margret's sudden stop and the way she yanked her hand from his arm almost made him stumble. Her sack started to topple, so he juggled it and prevented yet another tumble to the ground. Samuel watched as she stared off to the right. Immediate alarm emerged on her face and replaced the coquettish expression that had been there a moment before. He followed her line of sight and took note of a lady who resembled Margret in many ways, only without any trace of the child that shone from Margret's young face. As the lady stood outside of the silversmith's, he had no trouble deducing her identity.

Margret turned her gaze to him, all trace of open interest gone. "I do apologize, Mr. Lowe, but I must depart."

"But, why—"

Margret placed a hand on his arm, but with another glance past him, she removed it. "Please, Mr. Lowe. I am not at liberty to discuss anything further." She extended her hand toward him, and he took it. "I have enjoyed our conversation more than any other I have had recently, and I do thank you for saving me from both the unruly soldiers and that fall."

With no other choice than to allow her to depart, Samuel bowed over her hand. On impulse, he placed a quick kiss on the back of it. She gasped at the action but didn't pull away. For a fleeting moment, warmth once again crept into her eyes, but just as quickly, Margret composed herself and reached for the sack he held.

"Good day, Mr. Lowe."

With that, she was gone.

Samuel waited a moment for her to make an escape, but then he followed her progress as she headed for the silversmith's. He flicked his gaze to the lady who waited for

Margret only to be met with a dark and foreboding glare. For a brief second, he wondered why she should hold any animosity toward him. Then he remembered his incriminating uniform and silently chastised himself for placing Margret in such circumstances.

He watched as the woman he assumed to be Margret's mother started walking in the opposite direction. With lowered head, Margret followed. Just before they disappeared from view, Margret turned and sought him out. He raised a hand in acknowledgment and nodded. She returned the gesture then vanished from sight. All Samuel had was the memory of her smile and the touch of her hand in his to mark the moments they'd shared.

❧

After spending another hour walking the perimeter of the town green and weaving his way among colonists, Samuel turned on his heel and almost bumped into another soldier.

"Sergeant Atworthy." Samuel nodded in greeting.

"Lieutenant," the soldier acknowledged. "Did you learn anything interesting?"

Samuel looked over his shoulder toward where he had last seen Margret. Interesting? That was one way of putting it. But that wasn't what Charles wanted to know. Samuel faced the man and shrugged. The sergeant stood with a firm grip on the rifle resting in the crook of his left arm.

"Probably no more than what you and the other men have discovered. The colonists are up in arms over the recent taxation from Britain, and they are assembling men in Philadelphia to do something about it." He recalled how Margret had neglected to mention the meeting he knew the men in her family attended. Now he did the same with Atworthy.

Charles frowned. "Yes, and I wonder if these colonists are prepared for what might happen should the king's army decide to take action against them."

"I was speaking to some of them a little while ago about that very thing." Samuel refrained from providing names or identifying Margret. He didn't want anyone else to know about the connection he'd made to such an influential family. "Some do not seem overly concerned about the consequences."

"While others are proceeding with caution," Charles added.

"Yes. There does not appear to be a clear dividing line between the stirrings of possible dissenters and those who remain loyal to the Crown." Samuel thought of Margret's adamance about the loyalty of the men chosen to attend the secret meetings. It was clear those men sided with the colonists, but a good number of the townsfolk had yet to make up their minds. "Have you been able to ascertain the general feeling here in town?"

The sergeant formed his mouth into a tight line. The hopeful expression he'd worn disappeared into one of bleakness. "I am at as much of a loss as you are, Lieutenant. Corporal Montgomery and I walked the streets for hours today. No matter which side is heralded in the conversation, the emotions are heightened equally."

"Well, we had best determine something concrete if we are going to provide an acceptable report to Major Johnson."

Charles spread his arms. "There does not seem to be a concrete conclusion, sir."

Samuel silently agreed. Could anyone blame the colonists for being mixed in their feelings? For the majority of their lives, they had enjoyed the benefits of having a ruling power across the ocean. If not for the high cost of the war against the French and Indians fifteen years ago, the taxes wouldn't be necessary. At least that was what the British told them.

"Perhaps we should confer with others in our regiment here in town." Samuel didn't exactly relish that task, as it would only delay his true mission. He would much rather be back at his tent, composing a letter to General Maxwell with the Colonial army about his findings. The general would no doubt be pleased with the news about Margret's family and the influence they wielded.

"I will speak with Sergeant Wright and Corporal Withers."

"About?"

Sergeant Atworthy regarded him with a curious stare.

Samuel closed his eyes for a second and shook his head. "Oh, right." He composed himself. "Conferring with them on their findings."

The sergeant hesitated a moment. "Yes," he began in a drawn-out response, peering at Samuel with narrowed eyes. "You just suggested that we speak with other soldiers before returning to give our report."

"Right. I did." Samuel silently chastised himself for allowing his mind to wander from his present duties. The last thing he needed was suspicion from anyone in his regiment, least of all a lower-ranking soldier. "I was merely planning words for our report."

"Very good." Charles nodded, seemingly satisfied by the answer.

"How about we each speak with two others and report back in front of the tavern in thirty minutes?"

"Yes, sir." The sergeant saluted and left.

Samuel held his breath until Charles was at least ten yards away, then he expelled it. That was too close. He blamed his addlepated brain on the distraction that young Margret had provided today. Had he not gotten lost in thought about her and her family, he would have been able to maintain his wits throughout his conversation with Lieutenant Atworthy. He only prayed Charles would not give his slip a second thought.

"Pssst."

Samuel froze and searched the area to the left and right. Nothing. No one.

"Pssst. Samuel!"

Now *that* voice he recognized. He turned and peered into the shadows of the foliage at the edge of the Presbyterian Church property that bordered the haberdashery. The vague outline of man stepped out from behind the bushes.

"Thomas," Samuel called to him in an exaggerated whisper. "I almost forgot I told you to wait for me."

Thomas placed his finger to his lips and peered both ways down the street. He signaled for Samuel to come to him. When Samuel reached the edge of the bushes, Thomas grabbed his arm and dragged him into the shadows.

"What is all of this about?" Samuel looked around and saw no one within hearing distance. "And why am I whispering?"

"Because you never know who might be lurking around the corner."

Samuel almost laughed at Thomas's serious expression. His friend had the lurking part right. But they didn't have to worry here. The men in his British regiment were otherwise occupied, and most of the townsfolk were far enough away that they didn't prove a problem. That didn't stop Thomas from taking extra precautions, though.

"So, are you going to tell me why you feel the need for us to take up residence in the shrubbery? Or am I going to have to wager a guess?"

"I received a message from General Maxwell while you escorted your damsel in distress."

"The general?" It had to be important if his commanding officer had dispatched someone to town to find them. "Has there been a change of plans?"

"Not exactly."

"Do I have new orders?"

"No."

So Thomas was going to be evasive.

"Does General Maxwell have an issue with my work?"

Thomas shook his head. "He believes you have performed above reproach and stand as an example to others among our ranks."

Samuel groaned deep in his throat. "Thomas, I grow tired of these games. Please tell me about the missive."

The devious fellow had the nerve to smirk. If Thomas didn't answer soon, Samuel might be tempted to use other means of persuading his friend to talk.

"The general wanted us to know that there have been more serious developments up north and that you might be sent there to probe in and around Boston for General Washington." Thomas folded his arms across his chest. "Is that information satisfactory, *sir*?"

The emphasis Thomas placed on *sir* made Samuel grin. If Thomas was anything but one of his best friends, he might take issue with the hint of disrespect. But he knew his friend was only joking. Thomas had a hard time taking anything seriously—even when it included orders from a commanding officer. At least he kept things exciting.

"Will anyone accompany me?"

A smug look crossed Thomas's face. "The general is allowing you to choose your traveling companions. Three, to be exact."

Samuel stroked his chin, his fingers brushing over the stubble of whiskers that had appeared since he shaved that morning. "Three men, hmm?"

"That is what General Maxwell's note said." Thomas held it out for Samuel to see.

Samuel took it and read the brief message. "And I am permitted to select anyone I desire?"

"Yes."

Samuel felt a spark of mischief. "I believe Rowe, Jackson, and Harding would serve as excellent companions."

The smug look disappeared, and Thomas's shoulders dropped. "Yes." He swallowed. "Yes, sir. They are skilled marksmen and possess abilities along the trail that would serve you well."

"They would at that." Samuel paused and tapped his lips with his forefinger, all the while gauging Thomas's reaction. "But Jackson does not possess admirable conversational skills, and Rowe has a tendency to be too serious. Harding? He reminds me of a dog that will not leave your side. Loyal to a fault and quite the nuisance when it comes to his devout methods of protection."

As Samuel listed the negative aspects of the three men he'd mentioned, Thomas brightened.

"I can think of only one man I might want to have by my side. One man I can trust with my life."

Light entered his friend's eyes. "And who might that be, sir?"

Samuel extended his hand. "Would you perhaps be interested in the job?"

Thomas shook his hand with vigor, and a smile beamed on his lips. "I would sooner turn myself over to the British and the Hessians than deny your request."

The man had a flare for the dramatic. But there truly was no one better. Their fathers had served together in the French and Indian War, and now he and Thomas joined together against a common foe, doing what they could to right the injustice and help bring about a better life for them all.

"Then I suppose we should return to camp and notify General Maxwell of my selection." Samuel led the way out of the bushes, careful to not be seen associating with Thomas. If any of the men in his British regiment were to spot him, there would be no end to the questions that would ensue. He would have to make his visit to General Maxwell quick so he could still report to his commanding officer with the British troops before dusk. Hopefully he could also convince them his secondary position as a scout would serve them well up north, especially if he shared some of what he knew about the movement of the Colonial army. Otherwise, his assignment from General Maxwell might be short-lived.

"I believe Jackson and Rowe are still the best options to complete our entourage." Samuel turned toward Thomas. "What do you think?"

"That we should stop wasting time thinking and get started on our journey."

Leave it to Thomas to get down to the basics once his fun and games were complete. Samuel smiled. "I could not agree with you more."

A certain young woman, however, made him wish he hadn't agreed so quickly. He'd have to find a way to have a note delivered to her, informing her of his new assignment but assuring her of his return as soon as possible. At least that way, Margret would know he had thought about her enough to pen the message. Otherwise, she might think he wanted nothing more to do with her. And that couldn't be further from the truth.

three

April 1775

Margret could hardly believe the declaration emblazoned in bold black and white in the special edition of the *Wilmington Journal*. All winter long, tempers had been rising and unstable conditions had been reported from the northeast. Papa and Grandfather had told her an attack was inevitable, and she had even begun to imagine what would happen as a result. Nothing could have prepared her for the reality that struck in cold, hard truth.

And Samuel was right in the middle of the fighting.

His note in late August told her he had been commanded to go north near Boston and keep an eye on developments there. For the past eight months, Margret had made a point of learning what she could about what was happening. Despite the signs that seemed to predict this outcome, the announcement of the attack April 19 came as such a shock.

She sat back against the settee and stared toward the windows at the front of the house. The muslin curtains fluttered in the breeze that crept through the one-inch crack between the glass and the windowsill. Being able to look out upon their land was so much better than seeing only the diamond-paned glass they'd had the year before. She could see everyone coming and going and be aware of visitors approaching the house.

But no amount of clear glass could have prepared anyone for the surprise attack by the British.

How could England be so angered at the colonies? The

very country from which many of the colonists had come now attacked with brutal ferocity a little over three hundred miles from her home. If the gossip she'd heard in town was true, it wouldn't be long before the war came to them. The battles would be fought in their own hometowns and amidst their own families.

"Margret, have you seen—"

She looked up as Papa stepped into the parlor, his eyes focused on the paper she held in her hands.

"I see you are the guilty party who has stolen away with my newspaper."

A twinkle glimmered in his eyes, so he wasn't upset with her. However, he no doubt needed the newspaper to prepare for the upcoming assembly meeting. There would be talk of the battles at Lexington and Concord and the repercussions, but Margret wasn't sure how involved she wanted to be. She wondered only what Samuel was doing right now.

"I am sorry, Papa. But I could not resist when I saw the words fairly shouting at me." She turned on the settee to face her father and held back the tears that threatened to fall down her cheeks. "Is it true the British attacked the colonists and almost took them by surprise?"

Papa came to sit on the footstool next to her. He brushed his knuckles across her cheek then placed his palm against her head and attempted to comfort her without words. Several moments passed before he spoke.

"Yes." Sorrow filled his voice. "And if it had not been for Mr. Paul Revere, a loyal colonist who has spoken out against the unfair taxation by England, the colonists might not have been ready."

Paul Revere. Margret remembered reading about him in another article.

"What did Mr. Revere do?"

"He was out at night when he saw the redcoats approaching. So he got on his horse and rode as fast as he could toward town. Unfortunately, he was captured."

Margret inhaled a sharp breath. "Then how did he warn everyone?"

"His traveling companion, Dr. Samuel Prescott, escaped capture and rode ahead. He was the one who passed on Mr. Revere's warning."

"So the colonists were able to prepare for the attack?"

Papa offered a half smile. "Primarily, yes."

"What happened?"

He regarded her with a quizzical expression. "When did you develop such an interest in the growing tensions between the British and the colonists?"

Margret ducked her head. If she told him the truth, he might get suspicious. But she didn't want to lie. She also didn't want Papa to believe she was keeping company with a soldier serving the opposing side. With a shrug and hoping her face didn't betray her, she said, "A few months ago, I encountered a young soldier in town who knew a lot about many of the things I have heard you, Uncle Edric, and Grandfather discuss. He answered some of my questions and gave me much to ponder."

Just as she predicted, Papa's curiosity turned to skepticism. He folded his hands in his lap and leaned slightly away from her. "Does this young man have a name?"

Margret licked her lips and swallowed, attempting to bring moisture back to her mouth. "Samuel Lowe."

"And have you been keeping company with him since your encounter?"

"No. He was sent to Boston almost immediately after we met."

The moment the words were out of her mouth, she held her breath. She shouldn't have shared so much detail, but she always did have trouble being less than honest with her parents. Papa visibly relaxed, though, and Margret slowly expelled the air from her lungs.

"And how did you learn of his whereabouts?"

"He penned a brief note and had it delivered to me."

Lines formed on Papa's brow, and he pressed his lips into a thin line. "Was this the missive delivered to the house by the courier a few months back?"

Margret nodded, amazed he recalled such a minor detail. Then again, attention to detail was necessary in his line of work, building ships.

"And am I to understand that from one conversation, you have developed an insatiable curiosity about politics?"

"No, Papa. It is much more than that. The encounter with Mr. Lowe merely initiated the questions." Tucking her legs beneath the settee, Margret placed her hands in her lap and attempted to appear older. "So many of our friends and family are occupied with talking about the disagreements and speculating on the outcomes that I thought it might be wise to gain information, as well." She offered a teasing grin. "After all, I do not wish to appear uneducated, what with you and Uncle Edric and Grandfather Gustaf all upstanding members of our assembly."

Papa chuckled in response and chucked her chin. "Now, there is a glimpse of the Margret I know and love. I had begun to worry that someone had taken you captive and sent an imposter in your place."

"Oh, Papa." Margret waved her hand in the air and shook her head. "You do go on."

His expression grew serious, and he touched her cheek. "It is only because I fear my little girl is becoming a woman, and she will soon be gone from me."

The tears she'd kept at bay gathered with others at her

father's words. Moisture blurred her vision, and she blinked several times to clear it. Margret covered his hand with hers. "Papa, no matter what may come"—she put her other hand on his heart—"I will always be here."

Papa's eyes took on a faraway look. It was as if the weight of the world were upon his shoulders, and he saw no way to relieve himself of the burden. A moment later, he came out of his reverie and once again concentrated on Margret.

"What do you say we ask your mother if she is able to spare you so that you might ride with me into town?" A teasing gleam appeared. "I do believe Mrs. Thomason at the dress shop misses her visits with you after the long winter."

Another visit to town! Margret threw her arms around her father and gave him a warm hug. "I love you, Papa."

He returned the embrace and spoke against her braided hair. "And I love you, Margret."

Pushing himself to his feet, he extended a hand toward her. She took it as he drew her up to stand beside him.

"Now, let us go and speak with your mother."

❧

Margret stepped down into the dress shop. The familiar clang of the bell hanging above the door signaled her entry. She looked around the shop, soaking in the wide array of colors in both patterns and solids on a variety of fabrics. There was a walking dress, a tea dress, two ensembles for everyday wear, and a handful of other samples for whatever need Mrs. Thomason's clientele required. Mannequins she had recently purchased from France displayed the samples, with bolts of fabric set out in bins behind each model.

"Good afternoon, Mrs. Thomason."

The rosy-cheeked owner of the dress shop removed the pins from her mouth and took the thimble from her thumb. Her perfectly coiffed hair sat in contrast to her simple attire as she worked on a customer's order.

"Margret, my dear!" She came around the counter. "It is so good to see you."

"I have missed my visits as well, Mrs. Thomason."

The older woman grasped Margret's chin in her hand and gave her a scolding look. "And how often must I remind you that there are no formalities here? I do believe I have instructed you on more than one occasion that this *Mrs.* nonsense simply will not do."

Margret giggled as the shop owner released her chin. "I am sorry, Miss Ella."

Ella nodded with an air of finality. "There. That is preferable." She gave Margret a quick hug and stepped back. "Now, what do you say to a nice cup of hot tea while we visit? The weather outside is certainly warmer than it has been of late, but the chill in the air seems determined to remain and wreak havoc on our plans to enjoy the coming spring."

Oh, how much she missed coming into town and seeing Miss Ella. Her warm and accepting nature just bubbled with effervescent charm and appeal. And no one else in town served tea as delicious.

"Have you taken note of the new fabrics near the front of the shop?"

Miss Ella disappeared behind the curtain separating her private quarters from the main area.

Margret walked toward where Miss Ella pointed, but her eyes were deterred by the two gowns in front of one window. A beautiful taffeta and rich silk brocade draped and clung to the mannequins, showing off their elegance as the skirts trailed to the floor and a few inches beyond, while simple yet elegant stomachers and serge skirts with petticoats had been assembled on two form figures set out in front of the other window.

"When did you receive these?"

"The material and patterns arrived with the last shipment of goods that made its way down from a harbor in New York," Miss Ella called from the other room. "I have only just completed the stitching on them, so do be careful."

New York. That was where Samuel was from. Margret silently reprimanded herself for allowing her thoughts to latch onto him when she should direct her thoughts toward Miss Ella. She fingered one of the soft muslins.

"I have never seen designs such as these on any woman here in town. Are they new?"

Miss Ella approached to fluff out the taffeta gown. "Yes, they were patterned after the latest fashions in England, with similar ones for sale in the shops in New York for the past few months. Because so many harbors are turning away British ships, the merchants must find other ways of making a living. These fashions were a result of a merchant who traveled on his own to England and returned to sell what he acquired during his visit. Now, they have made their way here."

"But will not the recent battles near Boston impede further information from being gathered by visits across the ocean?" Margret reached for the hem of the gown and pulled it out to its full length, then she allowed it to flutter back into place. "It would be quite difficult to secure passage even along the rivers between colonial towns, let alone attempting to find a vessel willing to make a journey of that distance during times like these."

"You are absolutely correct, my dear. The fighting that—"

The hiss of boiling water from the teakettle in the other room caught Miss Ella's attention.

"Do allow me to tend to that, and we will continue our discussion in just a moment."

With cups in hand and settled at one of the working tables

in the shop, Miss Ella started the conversation again.

"Now, where was I?" She took a sip of the hot brew. "Ah yes, the fighting up north. You are correct in your observation that learning of the latest fashions and happenings in England will be quite difficult now. In truth, information has not been as forthcoming of late since the problems with the Sugar, Stamp, and Townshend Acts."

Margret nodded. Although she'd been only four years old when the Stamp Act passed, her family had been talking about the oppression by the British for as long as she could remember. And to think, Papa had served in aid of the British during the war against the French and Indians. How quickly things changed!

"I remember Papa talking about the massacre in Boston five years ago and how the mistrust of the British increased after that. Many did not relish the idea that they were taking up residence in our towns and becoming our neighbors at almost every turn." Margret inhaled the strong aroma of the fresh-brewed tea. She looked down into her cup and frowned. "And this." She gestured at the dainty cup she held, its filigree pattern simple yet striking in design. "Something in such high demand that the British wanted to tax it led to the protest just a year and a half ago where the colonists dumped all of that tea overboard into Boston Harbor."

Miss Ella sighed, her countenance taking on a more somber appearance. She set down her cup and held it between her hands. "Yes, we have met with a number of unfortunate incidents where the British are concerned."

"What I do not understand is how they could turn their backs on us in such an abrupt manner." Margret flattened her palm against the worn surface of the wooden table, feeling the small holes from when Miss Ella would use pins to hold a piece of fabric in place. "One minute, we are fighting on their side against the French, and the next, we are forced to abide by their unfair taxes and rule. We are not even permitted to have any say in the governing methods—methods decided by men who do not live here in the colonies."

"I am often in a quandary about it myself. I receive patrons of all kinds here in my shop. Some are in favor of continued British rule, while others are biding their time, waiting for the moment when they can be free from oppression." Miss Ella regarded Margret from across the table. She furrowed her brow and quirked her mouth. "And since when have you developed such an avid interest in the increasing conflicts between the colonies and the British?"

Margret's neck and cheeks grew warm under Miss Ella's perusal. She should have known the dressmaker would notice something different from previous visits. Before she met Samuel, the results of the meetings at the town hall and other gatherings of the assembly interested her only inasmuch as they provided details of the next social event to be held. Now she devoured every morsel of information she could find.

Miss Ella clapped her hands together, and Margret startled at the loud sound. "I know what has you so preoccupied."

Margret looked up. "You do?" Was she that transparent? She'd tried so hard to make her interest appear normal, but she obviously wasn't doing a good job. First Papa, and now Miss Ella. Even Mama had questioned her a few times throughout the winter when she caught Margret in a daydream.

"Yes. It is a young man, is it not?"

Margret tried to assume a detached air.

"I have not yet reached my fifteenth birthday, Miss Ella. With Mama grooming me to assume more responsibilities at home, I do not have the time for fanciful notions."

Margret took another drink of tea and hid the grin playing at the corners of her mouth behind the cup. Truth be told, she had spent more time thinking about Samuel than she had on her daily responsibilities—much to Mama's chagrin.

"Yes, and your birthday is only four months hence. You have recently been permitted to attend the balls held at the governor's home. Am I to assume that there has been no mention whatsoever of your seeking out a potential suitor in the next year?"

Miss Ella was obviously not fooled in the least. Margret tried to decide which way to take the conversation. Should she share the complete truth or stay closer to the side of ambiguity?

The muddled state of her mind won out. She needed to confide in someone, and with planting season well underway, Miss Ella seemed like the best person.

"Mama and Papa have remarked about my future."

"But there has been no talk about this young man who has vexed you to the point of distraction?"

"None of consequence," she answered without thinking. "I mean... That is..."

A look of triumph appeared on Miss Ella's face. "I thought as much."

The dressmaker stood and collected their empty teacups, then she reached beyond the curtain leading to her private quarters to deposit the cups before turning to face Margret once more.

"Working here in town affords me the ability to observe people in the most unique circumstances. It is quite amusing to see how honest and forthcoming women are when they are being fitted for new gowns." She pointed at Margret. "You, my dear, have shown me your feelings quite clearly, although I daresay the average person would not have deciphered the truth as easily."

Margret wrung her hands in her lap and gathered her petticoat in bunches. She had thought telling Miss Ella would be the best path, but now she was not so sure. What if Mama and Papa found out? Papa knew Samuel's name, and Mama would no doubt soon know that as well, but beyond that, Margret hadn't shared anything else.

The older woman approached and placed her hand on Margret's shoulder. "Do not fret, my dear. I promise that your secret is safe with me." She paused, and Margret looked up to find a reassuring smile on Miss Ella's face along with a mischievous gleam. "As long as you provide me with further details."

Something about the woman's nature comforted Margret and made her reservations fade away. She smiled and relaxed, untangling her hands from her petticoat.

"We met in late August last year when the three lawyers were preparing to journey to Philadelphia."

"Ah, so he lives here in New Castle?"

Margret looked down at her hands. "No. He came from New York, and now he is in Boston."

Puzzlement made Miss Ella's brow furrow. "What brought him this far south?"

"I believe he was here to observe the reactions of the colonists to the British imposing their unfair taxes."

The dressmaker gasped and covered her mouth with her hand. "Is he in favor of the British rule?"

If only she knew. Then she might not be so confused by everything. "I am not certain. We only spoke briefly, and he *was* dressed in a crimson uniform, but he did not look like the other British soldiers who were in town that day. His appearance was quite polished, but that could be because of his officer status."

Miss Ella nodded. "Yes, officers do set themselves apart from the other soldiers. But even officers in the Colonial army have been mistaken for British soldiers. Many of them maintain the dress and uniform of the British from the war with the French. I have even completed alterations on some at special requests. From looks alone, without the red coat, it would be almost impossible to tell them apart." She tapped one finger against her chin. "Did he say anything to you that would reveal his affiliations?"

Margret shook her head. "Nothing at all. In fact, he seemed to walk the line between the two sides without aligning himself to either one."

"And how do you know he is now in Boston?"

"He sent me a note before he left, promising to return as soon as possible."

"It appears as if this young man is smitten with you as well." The dressmaker smiled. "Otherwise, he would not have taken the time to pen the missive and make certain it was delivered to you."

Margret stood and walked over to one of the mannequins clothed in everyday walking attire. Mama had fashioned similar clothing for her just last summer. She'd worn it the day she met Samuel. "But if he is a British soldier, I must not encourage a relationship of any kind with him. And if he is a patriot but concealing his true alliance, how am I to trust him?"

"That does present a problem."

She turned to face Miss Ella. "Now do you see why I am so confused?"

The dressmaker approached and cupped Margret's chin with her hand. "I believe your confusion is a result of your attraction to this young man. Despite your brief introduction, he seems to have captured your affection. Only you can determine whether he is worthy of that affection." She released Margret's chin to enfold Margret's hands in her own. "Right now, it does not appear there is much you can do about your confusion. But if he has promised to return, you will have to wait until he does to decide where his loyalties lie."

Margret held the moisture at the corners of her eyes in check as she looked up into Miss Ella's motherly face. "And if they lie with the British?"

"That is a decision you, and you alone, will have to make."

Margret gave the dressmaker a hug and stepped back. "Thank you, Miss Ella. I am so glad Papa suggested that I come to town with him today."

"And is he at the town hall?"

"Yes. I am to meet him on the front steps at the conclusion of the meeting." She looked outside and took note of the position of the sun. "That is no doubt quite soon."

Gathering her reticule from the table, Margret headed for the front door.

"Guard your heart, my dear," Miss Ella called from behind her. "Deception can come in many forms."

Margret smiled as she reached for the latch. "I promise." She opened the door and looked over her shoulder. "And I will be sure to tell you the outcome when I see him again."

"Good-bye," Miss Ella called as Margret closed the door behind her and stepped onto the sidewalk.

A horse and carriage clip-clopped over the cobblestone street in front of her. The late-April sun shone bright in the clear sky above, but the cool breeze from the nearby Delaware River made Margret cross her arms to ward off the chill. She shaded her eyes and looked across the main square toward the town hall. The men were just leaving the meeting. Good. She wasn't late.

As she closed the distance between her and Papa, her thoughts returned to her discussion with Miss Ella. Would Samuel return as he promised, or would he forget all about her? If he did return, she would have to guard her heart as the dressmaker advised. At least until she figured out if she could trust him. And only prayer could help her make that decision.

four

May 1775

Samuel dropped the reins and allowed his horse to drink from the gurgling stream. He worked out the kinks in his back and stretched his legs as the water rushed and tumbled past on its way toward the river. Not even the rocks or stones impeded the flow. At times he felt just like that stream.

He'd been riding for what felt like days to his sore muscles. Just a few more miles, and he'd be close to New Castle again. His heart quickened at the thought of seeing Margret and instead concentrated on his orders, but it was no use. When Major Johnson told him the men from their regiment who had been sent north were returning to Philadelphia, Samuel inwardly rejoiced, even while he knew this meant they would be bringing their offense closer to the three southern counties of Pennsylvania. It had been almost nine months, and Margret's sweet face had never been far from his mind.

His time near Boston had been one of great success. His scout position had served him well with his British regiment. Only a select few had been ordered north. The rest remained behind to improve their firing techniques and overall battle strategies. His duties during this recent assignment often sent him ahead of the other soldiers or off on his own. He couldn't have gotten a better assignment. As he often did when he had the chance, Samuel bowed on one knee in the soft grass and tilted his chin heavenward.

"Thou most gracious Lord. It is with humble appreciation

and gratitude that I thank Thee for Thy protection and favor. Thou hast been my guide and covering through every obstacle. I know Thou hast called me to serve in this manner, and I vow to continually seek Thy wisdom and leading as I have always done. In Thy most precious name. Amen."

Far too often, Samuel had encountered situations that seemed impossible. With the good Lord at his side, though, he triumphed. Now, in the midst of what could be the most important task of his life, he relied on God that much more.

When Major Johnson had commended him for his skills in the recent battles up north, Samuel had almost broken down and confessed. He hadn't helped the British much at all. Being a spy came with risks, though, and they were risks Samuel was willing to take.

The call of a dove sounded in the trees to his left. His horse picked up his head and whinnied. Samuel reached for his reins and started to mount when the call sounded again. He looked to the branches nearby but saw nothing. On a hunch, he raised his hands to his mouth and answered back with a mimicked robin song. Sudden movement in the copse of trees caught his attention, and he immediately reached for his pistol.

"Samuel. Relax. It's me," came the whispered reassurance.

"Thomas?"

"Yes."

He should have known the identity from the dove call. That was a secret communication code they'd set up in case they might be followed. Samuel looked behind him and saw no one, so he waved Thomas forward.

"Where are Jackson and Rowe?" he asked when Thomas stood in front of him.

Thomas nodded over his shoulder. "They are lying in wait just over that hill. The rest of your British regiment is no more than twenty minutes behind you."

"Have you been trailing us since we parted ways in New York?"

"Yes." Thomas puffed out his chest for a few seconds, then he released his breath and looked Samuel straight in the eye. "I know you told us to go on ahead and rendezvous in New Castle, but Jackson and Rowe and I all agreed that you could benefit from a little extra protection." He grinned. "After all, we know how those British cannot be trusted."

"Yet somehow, I have managed to convince them that *I* can be."

Thomas clapped him on the shoulder. "That is because you are an expert at deception."

Samuel rolled his eyes. "Not exactly a trait I wear with honor, my friend." He sighed. "Although I must confess that I enjoy the thrill that accompanies the secrecy." *Even though it goes against everything I was raised to believe*, Samuel added silently.

"And were it not for that very skill, we might not have gained the advantage we secured at Ticonderoga earlier this month."

Thomas made a good point.

He acknowledged the statement with a nod. "Thanks to the loose-lipped confessions of a couple of officers, I learned of the poorly garrisoned situation at the fort."

"And because of that message you had delivered to Ethan Allen," Thomas continued, "he and his Green Mountain Boys from Vermont, along with Benedict Arnold, were able to capture the fort and take command of the stockpile of British weapons."

"I am relieved that the message made it to Allen. Not five minutes after I sent it, two men from my British regiment appeared from nowhere. They said Major Johnson had

requested I return and had sent them to search for me."
Samuel's breath quickened at the mere recollection of the
moment. "It was only my position as scout that saved me
from questioning as to why I was that far from camp."

Thomas draped his arm around Samuel's shoulders and
leaned in close. "But you survived, and the colonists secured
their first major victory of this war." He winked. "How does it
feel to have played a pivotal role in the success of the Colonial
army?"

Samuel shook his head. "Sometimes, Thomas, your antics
and exaggerations are beyond belief."

His best friend pulled away and crossed his arms. "But
think about how utterly tedious and dull your life would be
without me." Thomas jerked his thumb toward the hill to
their right. "Perhaps I should return to Jackson and Rowe,
where my antics would be better appreciated."

"And desert me to the mercy of my British regiment?"

"It would serve you right."

Samuel gave Thomas a smug grin. "You would never do
that, and you know it. As do I. So cease with your idle threats,
and let us continue on our journey."

Thomas relaxed his shoulders and dropped his arms to his
sides. "You are correct, as usual, my friend." He turned and
walked back into the protection of the trees, where he took
the reins on his horse and mounted. "I shall return to our
other compatriots over the hill yonder, and we shall make sure
you come to no harm." With a salute, he turned the horse
toward the southwest and spurred him into a gallop.

Once again alone, Samuel climbed onto his own mount
and headed back in the direction of his regiment. If Thomas's
guess had been correct, he should encounter them in just a
few minutes. From there they would head straight for the
outskirts of Philadelphia and Wilmington. And if he waited

for the opportune moment, Samuel could steal away to see Margret. He only prayed she'd be receptive to his arrival.

෨

The soft snores of the soldier next to him assured Samuel that he could escape the tent undetected. He penned a quick note that he was off again on another scouting mission and left the note on his bedroll. With slow and measured steps, he crept toward the flap at the entrance, taking care to maintain his balance as he waddled with knees bent, one step at a time. Just as he reached for the knot to loosen the tie, his tent mate's snores changed. Mumbling and the smacking of lips made Samuel freeze.

He waited a few extra moments after the man settled once more, then he resumed his course. In no time at all, he slipped out of the tent and ducked around the side to stay in the shadows. The last thing he needed was for the night watchmen to spot him moving about the camp. Major Johnson had asked that he keep this assignment between the two of them, which suited Samuel just fine. It wasn't long before the sun would rise, so he had to hurry.

Making his way toward the deeper part of the forest near where they'd made camp, Samuel gathered the belongings he'd stashed earlier. He would have made far too much noise had he left everything in camp and tried to get out, weighed down by his gear, without anyone hearing him. Once he was sure he had everything, he inched his way just inside the tree line toward the makeshift stables at the edge of camp. A soft whistle signaled his horse. The pacer grabbed hold of the rope that tied him to the post and, with deft skill, loosened the knot. Seconds later he was at Samuel's side.

"What a smart one you are," Samuel crooned in soft tones as he stroked the animal's forelock and nose.

After feeding a carrot to his horse, Samuel quickly adjusted the stirrups, tightened the cinch, and mounted. He guided the horse at a slow walk along the outside of the camp boundaries into the dark night. God had provided a few timely clouds that all but concealed the moon above, so his path remained hidden. When a branch snapped beneath the horse's hoof, Samuel pulled up on the reins, and they stopped. He looked over his shoulder for any movement, any sound. Nothing but the early morning calls of the crickets and other night creatures answered back.

Breathing a sigh of relief, he once again nudged Monticello into action. In no time at all, they were safe from detection, and the moon had moved from behind the clouds, shining a bright light on the path in front of them. Normally, gopher holes and other obstructions in the road might injure him or his horse but not tonight. Samuel gave Monticello his head, letting the horse gallop across the miles. He guided them in the direction of the Delaware River, which flowed south along the eastern sides of Wilmington and New Castle. If he stayed near the river, he could steer clear of any soldiers who might be camped farther inland.

Just as the first streaks of orange, pink, red, and yellow painted the sky in a rainbow of color, Samuel arrived at the edge of New Castle. On his way, he'd passed several farmers already at work in their barns, preparing for another day's labor. A handful of merchants were in their shops as well, getting an early start. He guided his horse along the cobblestone streets, and the first smells of fresh-baked bread reached his nose. Following the scent, he came upon the restaurant adjoining one of the town's taverns on Harmony Street. A handful of townsfolk were already inside, so he looped the reins around the hitching post and stepped inside.

"Good morning to you, sir." A middle-aged woman approached as his eyes adjusted to the dark interior. "My name is Constance Bedford. I am the proprietor of the Rising Sun. What can I serve you this morning?"

"Samuel Lowe, Mrs. Bedford." He tipped his hat, removed it, and tucked it under his left arm. "Might I sample a couple of eggs and some biscuits with gravy?"

"It would be my pleasure." Constance extended her arm in a sweeping gesture. "You may select any table you prefer. It is a bit too early for most of my regular patrons."

Samuel chose a small table by the window. Mrs. Bedford followed and filled the coffee cup in front of him.

"Your meal will be ready in a few minutes."

Once the proprietor left, Samuel took a moment to look around the restaurant. Tasteful decorations gave the room a comfortable atmosphere, while the well-worn planks of the hardwood floor and the scuffs in the main walking areas let visitors know this tavern was a favorite of the townsfolk.

He wondered if Margret ever came here with her family when meetings of the assembly were in session. Thoughts of her caramel locks drew his eyes to the coffee in his cup. Quite a bit darker than the tendrils he remembered, but the porcelain cup he held matched the pale smoothness of her cheek.

After the serving girl delivered his meal, Samuel tried to think of how he was going to see Margret. It wasn't as if she lived in town and he could walk up to her door. He more than likely wouldn't receive a warm welcome, anyway. Now that hostilities had begun, soldiers who didn't clearly align themselves with the Colonial army had a better chance of being tarred and feathered than welcomed. And he didn't exactly relish the idea of being made to look like a chicken.

Samuel finished his meal quickly, paid his bill, and exited the tavern. The sunlight blinded him for a few seconds, and he shaded his eyes as they adjusted to the bright outdoors. Horses' hooves clacked, and carriage wheels rumbled along the stones. In the distance, a dog barked, and the wind whispered through the leaves of the oaks and maples that lined the streets. It was almost June. The town was coming alive with the merchants, tradesmen, and other colonists who bustled about, everyone having somewhere to go.

Everyone but him.

He would have a place to go if he had taken the time to think out his plan better. But planning hadn't entered his mind, other than determining what he needed to do in order to complete the task Major Johnson had asked of him. He wanted to see Margret again, too—find out if the initial spark he felt when he saw her was still there. Only he didn't know how he would accomplish that and still see to his duties. There had to be a way.

Nothing would be accomplished by standing there, though, so he headed for the center of town, hoping someone or something might give him an idea. As he passed the Immanuel Church on Second Street, he thought about going inside and seeking the good Lord's help. Two well-dressed gentlemen in the middle of what appeared to be a private conversation caught his eye. Samuel assumed a nonchalant air and drew closer to them.

"Are you certain of this?" the man with jet-black hair asked.

"Yes." This came from the younger of the two, a man no less distinguished. "I received a letter from my cousin just yesterday. The delegates have gathered again in Philadelphia for a second meeting of the congress. This time, they intend to take a better plan of action against the British and attempt to organize the militia into some semblance of order."

"I must say, it is high time this happened." The older gentleman puffed out his cheeks and expelled his breath. "Despite the victory gained at Ticonderoga and the success we had with the minutemen keeping the British at bay in Concord, our men are still no match for the redcoats and their trained military."

"I agree," said the second. "And it appears as if the delegates we sent feel the same way. There has even been talk about making General Washington the commander in chief, but no decisions have been reached as of yet."

Samuel turned toward a low brick wall and propped his foot on the ledge. Retrieving a handkerchief, he started buffing his boot. He didn't want the two men to know he was listening, but he didn't want to miss hearing what they had to say.

General Washington, Philadelphia, and the gathering of the delegates at a second congress. He wondered if Major Johnson had received a similar message as that of the letter the second man's cousin sent. Or was it purely coincidental that his regiment had made camp between Wilmington and Philadelphia during this time? As happy as news of the progress the colonists seemed to be making made him, the threat of redcoat armies mounting surprise attacks on the colonists in this area worried him more.

"Did your cousin make any mention of any specifics the congress would be discussing?"

"Not in the letter, no," replied the second man. "But with Washington fighting the redcoats up north and our armies attempting to drive them into Canada or keep them from coming south, I would imagine talk of plans against attacks farther south might be of great importance."

"Our own assembly will be gathering midmorning to discuss that very thing. They met a fortnight ago, but no definitive conclusions were drawn. So McKean has requested that they convene for another meeting."

Midmorning! That news was music to Samuel's ears. Of course, a meeting didn't guarantee that Margret would accompany her father into town, but the possibility did exist. And Samuel wanted to make sure he didn't miss her if she came.

Making a final swipe of his handkerchief over the top of his boot, Samuel stuffed it back into his pocket and stood. Without looking in the direction of the two men, he made his way closer to the town hall and looked for a place to wait. It wouldn't be long before the assembly members started arriving.

∂⋅

Two hours later, a group of men in powdered wigs ascended the front steps of the town hall. Samuel came alert as he watched their entrance into the brick building. Fifteen minutes later, more men arrived, some wearing wigs and others with their hair pulled back simply in a pigtail. Considering the formal nature of these meetings, the lack of adherence to protocol made quite a point about the overall feelings of the colonists. He smiled despite the seriousness of the situation.

Just as he turned to watch the streets, his gaze settled on a wagon entering from the south side of town. From this distance, he couldn't be sure, but the hair color and approximate height of one of the occupants seemed to match. Then again, after nine months, Margret could have changed. He kept his eyes on the wagon, and as it drew up to the front of the town hall, his breath hitched.

Margret's father climbed down from the wagon and offered his hand to another young woman before extending his hand to help his daughter. Her uncle joined her father on the side closest to the hall. The men both said something to the girls, who nodded. A young lad approached and took charge of the wagon, but it was Margret who held his attention. She waved at her father and uncle and left their company to walk toward the center of town, the other young woman walking with her. When they reached the green, they paused and changed directions.

Straight toward him.

Samuel froze. Should he pretend to bump into her or purposefully make himself known? Would she recognize him if he did? What would he say to her? How would she receive him?

He didn't have time to come up with answers to his own questions. All too soon, she was no more than twenty-five paces away. Throwing caution to the wind, Samuel pushed away from the wall where he'd been leaning and stepped into the sunlight.

Margret turned her head and looked right at him. She stopped. Her gloved hand came up to cover her mouth, and her eyes widened. So she *did* recognize him. And she didn't run away. That was a good sign. Her companion touched Margret's arm and leaned close to speak. Margret shifted her gaze briefly and nodded, then she said something in return. A moment later, Margret's companion turned and headed back down Second Street, making a left turn at the corner and heading toward the river.

Samuel once again returned his gaze to Margret to find her watching him. Mustering what courage he had, he took the few steps necessary to close the distance between them. When they were standing face-to-face, he hesitated and drank in the sight of her. If it was possible, she was even more beautiful than he had remembered. The customary lappet cap adorned her curled locks, and a white apron with pink ruffles covered the front of her gown and petticoats.

When he returned his gaze to her face, a pink blush colored her cheeks, and her eyes were downcast.

He immediately removed his cocked hat and bowed. "Forgive me, Miss Scott. I did not intend to cause you discomfort."

She dipped her head but avoided his eyes. "No harm has befallen me, Mr. Lowe."

"How are you?"

"I am well."

Of course she was well. What else would she be? Samuel floundered for something to say that wouldn't make him sound like an uneducated schoolboy.

"Who was that young woman with you a moment ago?"

Margret glanced over her shoulder then back at him. "That is my cousin Julianna. She is seventeen and has offered to chaperone my visits to town."

Samuel regarded her in amusement. "It appears as if your cousin might be in need of instruction regarding the duties of a chaperone."

Margret reached into her pocket and withdrew a fan, which she snapped open, hiding her face as a musical giggle sounded from her lips. "Actually, she is well aware of the role she is supposed to be playing." She leaned forward, as if imparting a big secret. "But she is here to meet a beau. Accompanying me provides her with the perfect excuse."

"Ah." Samuel ran his tongue across the bottoms of his teeth. "Quite the charlatan, she is."

With a shrug, Margret replied, "As long as it remains innocent, I do not see the harm."

"Nor do I," Samuel was quick to agree, "but I daresay your father or hers would not be overly pleased to learn of this little deception."

Indignation leapt into Margret's eyes. "Uncle Jurien is aware she has a beau, but he does not know how often she sees him. Before long, they will be betrothed, and it will no longer matter."

Samuel extended his hands in a placating gesture. "Do forgive me, Miss Scott. I did not intend to offend you."

She immediately became penitent. "And do forgive me, Mr. Lowe, for allowing my temper to get the better of me."

"Consider it done." He shifted from one foot to the other. "Now, what brings you to town this fine day?"

"Papa and Uncle Edric are here to attend a meeting." She grinned. "I asked if I could come into town to seek respite from the labors of the second part of the planting season, but I might see if I can purchase a new set of mitts."

Samuel regarded her in silence. It appeared her interests remained in clothing and fashion.

"When did you return from the north? And what brings you to New Castle today?"

You, he almost said, but he held his tongue. "I returned only three days past with the men who accompanied me to Boston last fall. Today I am on a mission for my commanding officer but decided I needed a change of scenery from the camp just north of Wilmington, so I rode a little ways south, and here I am."

He wished he could tell her the whole truth, but he needed to gain her confidence first.

"Did your time spent up north meet with success?"

"In some ways," he answered. "In others, it became clear that more planning was needed to complete the mission."

A couple approached, and Samuel unconsciously stepped closer to allow them to pass. Margret gasped and stepped back, causing the woman to turn her head and look at the two of them.

Samuel cleared his throat. "Will you walk with me?" He extended his arm.

She hesitated only a moment before tucking her hand into the crook of his elbow and turning in the direction he led them. Several moments passed in silence, and Samuel took note of the dressmaker's shop to their right, followed by the apothecary. As they headed toward the river from Second Street, the silence nagged at him.

"I must say, it is a pleasure indeed that you have come to town today. When I decided to venture this far south, I cannot lie and say it was not without the hope of seeing you again."

Margret lowered her eyes and looked away. "I wondered if you would indeed return like you promised in your note."

She spoke the words so softly that Samuel wasn't sure he heard her correctly. When she raised her head to look at him, though, he knew what he'd heard was right. He smiled.

"One thing you will never have to doubt, Miss Scott, is that I always keep my promises. On that, I pledge my troth."

A contented expression crossed her features. "How long will you be staying this time?"

He sighed. "I wish I knew." Weighing his words carefully, he continued. "If the outcome of certain decisions goes one way, I could remain in this area for several months." A hopeful light entered her eyes. "But should the outcome go the other way, it might mean I will be called upon to disappear, for all intents and purposes, for quite a while."

Disappointment quickly replaced the hope, and a frown marred her pretty features. "And will those decisions be in favor of the British or the colonists?"

The wariness in her eyes gave Samuel pause. He didn't know which way to answer. One would ensure that she would never speak to him again. The other would only be telling a half-truth. Weighing his options, he felt compelled to be honest. There was no other way he could gain her trust. And by doing that, he would gain access to potential information both sides desperately needed. Her father would be aware of the ships in the river between here and Philadelphia, and her uncle would know of the local plans to thwart the British advance. It was a relationship he couldn't afford to jeopardize. And it didn't hurt to have such a charming young woman to aid his cause.

With a sigh, Samuel looked down into her upturned face.

"Before I answer that question, I must ask you to promise me you will listen to the end before passing judgment."

Margret regarded him for several heartbeats, then she nodded. "I promise."

"I am a soldier with Major Johnson's army, currently camped between Wilmington and Philadelphia and preparing for battle." She gasped, but he continued. "I serve the major as both a soldier and a scout. Both of those positions enabled me to journey north with a small company of British soldiers and be part of the battles outside of Boston."

She turned away and stared straight ahead, but he could see the sadness reflected in her profile. He didn't relish the idea of upsetting her, but she had to know everything about his line of work—not only the parts she wanted to hear. This next part was sure to change her countenance.

"But I also serve General Maxwell with the Colonial army as a spy."

At this, Margret stopped in the middle of the street and tilted her head to look at him. Samuel caught himself before he tripped, then he turned to face her.

"A spy?" Her eyes widened as the truth of his words seemed to penetrate her conscience. "So, you wear the uniform of a British officer but actually support the colonists?"

"Yes."

She gave him a cursory glance from head to toe. "But you are not wearing your uniform now."

"I am on a scouting mission for Major Johnson. And with feelings being what they are, it would not be wise for me to be seen wearing the telltale coat to identify me."

"Ah, yes. You are correct."

He shrugged. "Of course, the location of my assignment just happened to be convenient enough to New Castle for me to pay this charming town another visit."

Margret quirked one corner of her mouth in an appealing way. "Then it is fortunate I was able to get away from my duties at home to be here today."

The coquettish behavior had returned. Samuel dipped his head and smiled. "It is, indeed."

She started walking again, leaving Samuel to quickly take the lead.

"So you returned to New Castle to scout for possible camp locations?"

"Actually, I am scouting colonist movement in this area." At her concerned reaction, he hurried to reassure her. "But of course, I will only tell them what they want to hear and refrain from revealing the actual plans made. General Maxwell has asked that I do what I can to keep the British closer to Philadelphia."

She brightened at this and tightened her grip on his arm. "Philadelphia is where the delegates are meeting again for the second congress."

So the information he'd confirmed today wasn't new— unless, of course, she had just learned it from her father.

"That is what I hear, yes." He nodded and guided her around a spot on the sidewalk where the brick had buckled. "And the meeting today"—he tipped his head in the direction of the town hall—"is for the men here in town to discuss ways to keep everyone here safe should the British bring the war farther south."

"I overheard Papa telling Mama that last night."

They had come to the edge of the river, and several others strolled along the banks or the pathways nearby. Samuel noticed Margret's cousin heading in their direction. When she reached them, instead of pausing for an introduction, she merely nodded at Margret and continued past. Samuel glanced over his shoulder to see her stop a few paces behind and turn to follow, maintaining a respectful distance. Good. She was again providing a chaperone for them. He certainly didn't need any wagging tongues adding to his already precarious situation.

Samuel turned to face Margret, pleading with his eyes. He clasped his hands in front of him to keep from reaching for hers. "Miss Scott, do forgive me if I am being too forward, but I find that even in the short time we have known each other, I am drawn to you." A rosy hue stained her cheeks. "I realize there are more than a handful of years between us, so for now, might you agree that we can be friends?"

She beamed, and the expression transformed her face. "That would please me greatly, Mr. Lowe."

For a moment, Samuel almost forgot their age difference. He could see evidence of the beautiful woman she would become, but for now, he forced himself to remain somewhat distant.

"Splendid. Miss Scott, I wish that I could tell you everything about what I do, why I am here, and my mission." He looked away and saw several boats traveling upriver. "But I cannot."

Margret placed a hand on his arm, and he relished the comfort the gesture offered. "Mr. Lowe, I understand the need to keep certain things confidential. And I promise not to press you for more than you are able to share. Should my curiosity get the better of me, I will not take offense if you must avoid answering my questions."

Samuel couldn't find the words to form a reply. He looked down at her open and trusting expression, encouraged at how easily she agreed to take him at his word. Breezes from the river blew around them and stirred the loose tendrils of hair at the nape of her neck. The lace edge of her lappet cap fluttered as well. She had changed so much since he last saw her—mature and more aware of the importance of the events taking place around her. But she was still young. He had to remain mindful of that fact.

He bent at the waist slightly and held the fingertips of one of her hands between his thumb and fingers as he captured her gaze. "Miss Scott, I cannot tell you how happy I am to hear you make that promise. And in return, I shall make a promise of my own. In due time, I promise to tell you everything about my duties. For now, despite what you may learn or hear about me, I must ask that you trust your heart before forming any conclusions."

He brushed the pads of his thumbs across her knuckles and inwardly thrilled when she shivered. Whether from his touch or the cool breeze, Samuel couldn't say for certain, but in his mind, it was the former.

"Wherever my duties take me, be it to remain here or be gone for a while, I will get word to you so you do not have to worry." Now he had to ask the difficult question. After only two meetings, for some, it might seem too soon. But for him, it felt like long enough. "Should I be called away, will you still be waiting when I return?"

"Yes," she answered without hesitation.

Samuel smiled and gave her hand a quick squeeze. "Miss Scott, your response has pleased me greatly. I know I do not offer much, but—"

Margret placed a finger to his lips. "But your loyalty to the cause you serve has more than convinced me of your true heart. I need nothing further on which to base my promise."

Samuel bowed over the fingers he lightly held. "Then for now, I shall return you to your errands. Parting ways will not be such a daunting task."

With Margret's cousin following, they returned to the center of town in silence. But words were not needed. He only prayed the path they were on would lead to an end filled with hope, not sadness.

five

Margret walked through the kitchen and headed outside toward the barn. The late August sun beat down upon her, but it wasn't any cooler inside. Beads of sweat trickled down her neck. She stopped at the doorway to the barn and dipped her handkerchief into a bucket of water left by one of the farmhands, relieved when the refreshing coolness hit her wrist. She leaned back against the large door of the lower level and, eyes closed, brought her handkerchief to her neck. The cloth offered a reprieve from the heat—no doubt more than what the men in the militia and Colonial army endured as they fought against the British onslaught.

Three months had passed since she last spoke with Samuel, and he had made no effort to contact her or be seen anywhere in town. The war raged on, just like her hope that she would receive word from the soldier who occupied her thoughts day and night. So far the battles had remained to the north of them, but that could change at any moment. Margret wondered if Samuel had been sent north as he had a year ago, then she remembered that he'd promised to let her know if his duties would take him away from her for long periods of time. That didn't stop her desire to see him or hear from him, though. And the not knowing was at times more difficult than the separation.

The last she'd heard, most of the fighting remained concentrated near the Canadian border. Papa had said there were even rumors of attempts to make Canada a fourteenth colony, but so far, there had been no progress. This tactical strategy followed on the heels of the British seizing control of Boston and sending the Colonial army into retreat. When Papa had told her about the battle at Breed's Hill just two days after General Washington had been named commander in chief of the entire Colonial army, she was certain she would receive a letter from Samuel telling her he had to leave again. Two and a half months later, and still nothing.

The sound of clanging metal made Margret crack open her eyes a slit to see her younger brother shaping a horseshoe as Papa watched. The pride on Papa's face was clear as he watched his eldest son work with iron. It wasn't often that Papa had the luxury of spending an entire day at the farm, but when he did, he made sure it was productive. Margret was pleased that her father had become one of the best ironworkers among the shipbuilders in Wilmington, and now it looked as if Nicholas would be following in his footsteps. Andrew and Micah, at nine and six, were still too young to start learning the trade, but if Papa had his dream, all three of his sons would join him.

She pushed away from the door and took several steps in their direction. Papa looked up when she approached.

"Be careful you mold that shoe just right, Nicholas," Margret couldn't resist teasing. "You do not want the horse to kick you because the shoe does not fit."

Nicholas paused with the hammer over the anvil, where he held the shoe. His gaze shifted to the hot coals and the iron in the fire next to him before returning to her. Guessing where his thoughts lay, she grinned and winked.

"You might want to be careful what you say, Margret," Papa warned, "especially when a man has a wealth of weapons within easy reach."

"Nicholas would never truly harm me, Papa." Margret kept her eye on her brother, who grinned despite returning his attention to his work. Thirteen years old, he already stood a few inches taller than she. She cast a sideways glance at Papa and gave him what she hoped was an angelic expression. "Besides, I have you to protect me."

Papa held up his hands in mock surrender and shook his head. "Do not rely on me to keep you safe if you are at fault for instigating the action." He placed a hand on Nicholas's shoulder. "I will not step in between the harmless antics of a brother and sister."

"And that means I would be well within my rights to teach you a lesson for taunting me," Nicholas added without lifting his head.

Margret placed her hands on her hips, her mouth open. "Do you mean to tell me that the two of you are forming an alliance against me?"

"Yes," they answered together.

Papa chuckled, and Nicholas smiled.

Margret huffed. "It appears my presence is not desired."

"On the contrary." Nicholas stopped again and gave her a direct look. "It is your interruption and distraction that are unwanted. I must concentrate on what I am doing, and I cannot do that if I am silently plotting how I can exact revenge against you."

Her brother delivered the remark with such a straight face, Margret had a difficult time determining whether he was joking or serious. She looked at Papa, who shrugged and said nothing, then she returned her gaze to Nicholas. A twitch at the corner of his mouth gave him away.

Just as she opened her mouth to reply, Mama called from the kitchen door.

"Margret!"

She pressed her lips into a tight line and glared at her brother. Nicholas laughed and began pounding the horseshoe again.

Margret turned toward the house. "Yes, Mama?"

"If you have successfully cooled yourself, your sisters and I would like to have your assistance with the pies."

"I shall come straightaway."

Papa jerked his head over his shoulder. "It is best that you *do* get back to the house, Margret. We might be preparing a dinner in honor of your fifteenth birthday, but that does not excuse you from doing your part to assist in the preparations."

Margret nodded. "I know, Papa." She turned to go but couldn't resist one parting remark. "Make certain Nicholas does not mistake his thumb for the horseshoe. It would be a travesty to introduce my younger brother as having only four fingers."

The low-throated growl from Nicholas made Margret giggle as she walked away. She had gotten the last word. That didn't happen very often, but when it did, she enjoyed every minute of it.

After cleaning the dirt from her shoes, Margret opened the back door and stepped into the kitchen. It felt twenty degrees hotter, and she had already shed as many petticoats as was proper.

"Thank you for coming so quickly." Mama smiled her appreciation and brushed the back of her flour-covered hand across her forehead. "Your sisters have brought more berries, and with the first ripe apples you picked this morning, we will have more than enough pies to feed everyone."

Margret looked at the far end of the table where eleven-year-old Lydia separated out equal amounts of blueberries and raspberries with painstaking care. Even five-year-old Abigail lent what help she could to the task. From the looks of her face, though, it seemed as if she was eating more than she was setting aside for the pies. By the end of September, one of Margret's favorite times of year, they would be close to having their final harvest of corn, peaches, and beans, all of which would be preserved. But for now, they had pies to make.

Margret stepped up to the table in the center of the kitchen and reached for an apple to begin preparing it for baking. "Is everyone truly going to come to the dinner tomorrow?"

Mama looked up from the dough that she flattened and smiled. "Everyone, my dear. Your four aunts and uncles, far too many cousins for me to count, and of course, all of us who live here."

At least she wouldn't have to worry about prospective suitors also in attendance. Unlike several of her friends who lived on Water Street in New Castle, her parents had not begun to pressure her into showing an interest in finding a suitable beau to come calling. Now that she was fifteen, though, there would no doubt be talk. A small part of her hoped to be able to introduce Samuel at that time, but without word from him, she had no way to extend an invitation.

Several hours passed as Margret and her sisters worked side by side with Mama. When she pulled the pies from their new Dutch oven, the aroma made the long hours they'd spent preparing everything worth it. Once the pies were set to cool, Margret left the heat of the kitchen for the cooler rooms in the house. As she passed through the parlor and glanced out the front windows, she saw a lone rider coming down the lane from the main road.

Now, who could that be this late in the afternoon?

Margret changed direction toward the front door and opened it in time to see Abel, one of the servants, accept a letter from the young man on horseback. The two nodded, and the rider left in the direction he'd come. The servant came toward the house and held out the letter when his gaze met hers.

A letter? For her?

With trepidation, she took the letter and nodded her thanks. After Abel left, she could only stare at the missive she held. Recognizing the slightly familiar scrawl of Samuel's pen did nothing to offset the heaviness of her heart as she realized this note meant she would not be seeing him as she had hoped.

Squeals and laughter sounded from the side of the house. Margret startled out of her stupor and looked up in time to see little Abigail running away from Nicholas and Andrew, who held large buckets of water and were chasing their sister, getting more water on themselves than on Abigail. Abel would no doubt notify her parents of the letter, but for the moment, she could keep it to herself. She clutched the message to her chest and headed toward the benches tucked in the small copse of trees off to the right of their house.

Once sure she was alone and away from prying eyes, Margret broke the seal on the single sheet of paper and read:

22 August, 1775

Miss Scott,

I am truly sorry that I shall not be there to deliver this in person, but as predicted, I have received orders to accompany many other soldiers and concentrate our efforts along the St. Lawrence River in New York and along the Canadian border. The fort on Lake Champlain and many sites in and around Quebec have been reported to be the central locations for most of the conflicts. As unpredictable as war is, though, the outcomes are left up to providence.

Despite every attempt I made to journey south, I was unable to return to New Castle as I had hoped. My orders do not tell me how long I will be away, but rest assured knowing that you will be in my thoughts while we are apart. I will be counting the days until I can see you again, and I hope you will do the same. Until then, I remain fondly yours.

Lieutenant Samuel Lowe

A sigh escaped Margret's lips. He had written this note six days ago and no doubt was well on his way to or had already arrived at his destination. She noticed that he didn't reveal his loyalties in any way through the words he had penned. He was doing an excellent job of straddling the two sides. And if she had to guess, his skills served him well as he kept everyone else guessing, too.

But what occupied her mind the most was knowing that she faced a long and lonely winter without the possibility of seeing him. Living on a farm helped some, as plenty would keep her busy, but it wouldn't keep her busy enough. With the letter pressed against her heart, Margret closed her eyes.

"Most Gracious Lord," she prayed in earnest. "I beseech Thee on behalf of my dear friend. Thou knowest the path he will take as he journeys with other soldiers and fights in the battles that are happening this day. Please place Thy hand over him and protect him from harm. I cannot offer any more than this, but Thou hast promised to hear our prayers. I place his safety in Thy hands this day. In Thy most holy name. Amen."

When Margret opened her eyes, a sense of peace settled around her. She had done all that she could and knew it would be enough. Now all she had to do was wait.

≈

Six weeks later, the end of harvest came, and Margret launched into the preservation process with renewed vigor. Each week that passed and each barrel, earthenware jar, and crock they stored brought Margret closer to when Samuel would return. With gratefulness for a bountiful crop, Margret's family gathered in mid-November for a day of thanksgiving where they praised God for the abundance and spent the day fasting to show their thanks.

The shipbuilding business slowed during the colder months,

but Papa kept busy with meetings of the assembly in town. And as usual, he brought reports home of the topics discussed or the decisions reached. The few tidbits he shared helped dispel the gloominess of winter and the turning over of another year. Hearing the news—no matter how sketchy—made her feel closer to Samuel.

Winter faded into spring, earmarked only by the return of slightly warmer temperatures. It wasn't until Papa came home with details of the successful capture of Montreal the previous November and the evacuation in March of the British troops in Boston, however, that Margret wanted to hear everything Papa had to say.

"It appears as if Mr. Paine's writings published in January have invigorated the spirits of our fellow colonists. And with the authorization from the congress in Philadelphia to establish the American navy, our privateers can now interrupt British trade and aid our patriots fighting on land."

Mama came up behind him and placed her hands on his shoulders. "Is there any part of you that misses the opportunity to go into battle?"

Papa tilted his head and peered at his wife. With his right hand covering hers, he smiled. "My place is here at home with my family." He turned and regarded each one of his children in turn as they gathered around the table for supper. "Keeping watch over the ports at the river to ensure the British do not break through is more important to me for the protection of all of you than fighting against the redcoats far from home."

Margret observed the unspoken communication between her parents, and her thoughts shifted to Samuel. She hoped one day she would find a man who would love her as much as her father loved her mother. It was too soon to know if that man might be Samuel, but she wouldn't mind if he was. The middle of April, and she wondered how much longer it would be before he returned. Two years in a row, they had been apart for nearly nine months between their meetings. It reminded her a little of her parents, only they had been separated by years during the war with the French and Indians. At least Margret had been able to see Samuel more often than that.

"How many have had the opportunity to read Mr. Paine's writings?"

Nicholas's voice brought Margret back to the present. She looked to Papa and waited for his answer.

"Because it was published as a pamphlet and not a book, the distribution was wide and well received. Thomas Paine is a passionate man who is quite adamant about the rights of the colonists and freedom for these colonies."

Margret spoke up next. "And do you think these writings will assist the Colonial army in defeating the British?"

Mama took her seat at the other end of the table and began passing the bowls for everyone to fill their plates. Papa took one bowl and gave Margret his undivided attention.

"It is difficult to say what the outcome of this war might be, Margret, but if the meetings at the town hall are any indication, the British do not know the depth of determination that exists in the men they are trying to conquer."

Margret smiled. "And if the men fighting against the British are anything like you, Papa, the British should raise the white flag of surrender now and save themselves the trouble."

Mama chuckled but quickly covered her mouth and held back her laughter. Papa merely winked.

"You seem to have developed quite an interest lately in the proceedings of the assembly and the progress of our militia out in the field." An amused expression crossed his face. "Perhaps if you conduct yourself properly, I might permit you to be present at the meeting next month here at the house."

"The members will be meeting here?" Margret almost

bounced in her seat, but she refrained from any outward show of emotion.

"Yes, but whether you will also be present remains to be determined."

"I shall endeavor to please you, Papa, and thank you."

This could be a fantastic opportunity. She would learn so much about what was happening. Were it not for Samuel's involvement, she might only concern herself with the minimum details needed to stay abreast of developments. But now, so much more was at stake.

She could hardly wait for the day of the meeting to arrive.

⋅ঽ⋅

Representatives from all over New Castle County arrived on horseback, by carriage, and on foot. Margret watched from the window in the kitchen, thrilled that the day was finally here. She had been restive for the past four weeks. Her excitement wasn't missed by Mama, who told of a time when she, too, had been permitted to listen to a meeting in the very same room. The two had shared a special moment as they realized the similarities in their situations.

Papa and Uncle Edric had been talking together with Grandfather Gustaf more often than usual, and from what Margret could gather, it sounded as if this meeting might be about more than just the war. They might also be discussing the possibility of breaking free from Pennsylvania and becoming a colony of their own.

Oh, how she wished that would happen! Not only would it provide them with their own governing laws but New Castle would become the center of it all. Right now, Philadelphia was the seat of ultimate control. Bringing everything closer to home would mean Papa might be able to consolidate more of his business with the shipbuilding industry in Wilmington instead of being forced to report to the overseeing parties in

Philadelphia every month. She knew Mama would be happy with that, and so would all of the children.

As Margret awaited Papa's call to the main hallway where she would be able to listen to the proceedings, restlessness sent her outside for a quick visit to the barn. The familiar smells greeted her before she set foot inside the wide double doors of the lower level. Movement to her left caught her eye, and she would have screamed had it not been for the hand that clamped over her mouth. A second later, an arm snaked around her waist and held her in place. She startled to struggle but stopped when her captor spoke.

"Miss Scott, please do not be alarmed," a familiar voice whispered next to her right ear.

She relaxed, and so did his hold.

"Now, do you promise you will not scream?"

She nodded and waited for him to remove his hand. As soon as he did, she turned, and he stepped around to face her.

"Mr. Lowe!"

He was again dressed in common attire, but even his every-day appearance held an air of superiority. Perhaps that worked to his advantage.

"I apologize if I startled you, Miss Scott, but I did not want you to alert anyone of my presence."

"You are forgiven, Mr. Lowe, but I must ask." She quirked one side of her mouth into a grin. "Shall we always find ourselves meeting in this manner, or will there come a time when you will not catch me by surprise?"

He smiled and bowed. "It is my hope, Miss Scott, that one day I shall be free to come calling without the concern over my own welfare or yours. But until that time, I am afraid we must be careful."

Despite her initial reservations regarding the secrecy, the thought of clandestine meetings gave Margret a small thrill.

Knowing she had to keep their relationship a secret, however, meant she would have to lie if someone asked her directly. And lying was something she simply didn't do.

"Would it be permissible to mention our friendship to Mama and Papa? They are already aware of the two messages you had delivered. If I were to refer to you as a friend, any time we spend together will not give them as much cause for concern."

"I see no reason why that would be a problem." A warning look preceded his next words. "But do be careful not to reveal too much about my line of work, or it might compromise my situation."

She nodded. "I promise."

Relief settled inside of her, and her breathing returned to normal. At least she didn't have to concern herself with keeping her entire relationship with Samuel a secret.

Samuel peered around the open doors of the barn and nodded toward the main house. "Am I correct in assuming a meeting is about to commence at your home?"

"Yes, and Papa promised me that I would be permitted to listen to the proceedings." She gasped and clapped a hand over her mouth. "Oh no!"

"What is it?"

"Papa."

"What about him?"

"He was going to come to the kitchen when the meeting was about to begin. If he already came and found me gone, he might have signaled the speaker to begin the meeting without me."

Samuel extended his hand. "Then shall we make our way toward the house where we might better position ourselves for adequate eavesdropping?"

Perceiving his teasing, Margret placed her hand in his and relished the safe feeling it gave her. "We shall, Mr. Lowe," she said as Samuel first made certain the path was clear before leading her toward the far end of the house and to a place concealed behind some rather tall bushes.

Margret didn't question how he knew where the meeting was taking place. If he had been there for even fifteen minutes, he no doubt would have overheard one of the men mention it. Right now, she simply enjoyed being with him and looked forward to hearing what the men inside would have to say.

"Now that we have reviewed and agreed upon the measures we shall take to protect our loved ones, let us proceed with the next order of business on the agenda." Margret recognized the voice of Thomas McKean. "That of establishing ourselves as a separate and individual colony."

So, they had already moved past the first order of business. It seemed they were going to make this meeting a quick one.

"Papa and Uncle Edric have been talking about this for several weeks," Margret whispered to Samuel, whose attention was fixed on the window above them. "Many of the residents in these counties have wanted this for a long time. Now it seems as if it could become a reality."

Samuel didn't acknowledge her words. She gave his arm a squeeze, and as he turned to look at her, she could see he was paying closer attention to the meeting than he was to her. When she didn't say anything, he looked back at the window again. That made her wonder about how he came to be here at her house on the very day the meeting was taking place.

This time she squeezed harder and earned a glare in response. Narrowing her eyes, she regarded Samuel carefully.

"How did you come to learn the location of this important meeting today?" Without giving him a chance to answer, she continued. "Did you come only because your duties required it? And will you now return to your camp and report what you learned today?"

Her questions obviously struck a nerve, for he cast a longing glance toward the window before giving her his full attention. He took several moments before replying, and resignation crossed his features before he spoke.

"Miss Scott, I told you early last summer that the work I am doing was not something I could share with you at this time. A year has passed since I shared that with you, but the situation has not changed."

"Well, if our friendship is to continue, then I believe you at least owe me the courtesy of sharing the reason for your visit today." She folded her arms. "You asked me to trust you. But how am I to do that unless I am certain that at the core of the choices you make, a purity of heart is driving those decisions?"

Samuel sighed. "Miss Scott, you can be certain that what I do, I do because I truly believe it is the right and necessary thing to be done. The good Lord has granted me certain skills, and I feel deep down that He has called me to serve in this manner. My purpose is what guides my actions, and that purpose is driven by the belief that I am doing what I have been called to do." He held out his hands, palms up. "More than that, I cannot offer. And only you can decide if it is enough."

Margret regarded him for several moments, and although she could tell he had once again turned his ear toward the window, his gaze never left hers. His deep brown eyes pleaded with her to trust him, and the words he spoke sounded sincere. But how could she be sure?

Trust me.

The silent words seemed to whisper across her heart as she closed her eyes and attempted to reason with all that Samuel had said. She had a choice to make, and the outcome of that choice would determine whether Samuel would continue to seek out her company or become nothing more than a memory. The latter thought caused a feeling of sadness to take hold of her.

Margret didn't know what it was about Samuel that compelled her to believe in him, but she knew that saying good-bye would bring her nothing but sorrow. Following her instincts and her heart, she made her choice.

"Very well." She unfolded her arms and waited to be certain he was listening. "I told you last year that your devotion convinced me of your loyalty and that I needed nothing more. I hold true to that with a fervent prayer that should you prove yourself to the contrary, I will be able to recover from your deception."

An earnestness appeared on Samuel's face, and he reached for her hands. "Miss Scott, I shall do everything in my power to make certain you do not experience any measure of disappointment where I am concerned. Your trust in me is not taken lightly, I assure you." He offered her a lopsided grin. "Now, may I ask that we continue to follow the proceedings of the meeting without further interruption?"

How could she say no to a face like that? The boyish features danced in contradiction to the firm jawline that gave evidence of the man who sat on his haunches before her. Whatever happened between them, should circumstances force her hand, Margret knew she would find it very difficult to walk away from him with her heart intact—for she feared it was already lost.

six

Samuel crept along the road that led to Strattford House but continued past the entrance and headed toward the designated place Margret had asked him to meet her. An iron bench that had been molded and shaped with painstaking detail, then whitewashed, sat amongst the concealing growth of the oaks and maples. The dense cover offered by the towering trees provided the perfect location. He hoped she could get away to join him here.

He stood for several minutes and listened. Nothing more than the soft rustling of the leaves as the wind blew through the branches and the occasional call of a robin or wren to his mate interrupted the peaceful hideaway. The snap of a branch made him whip around to identify the intruder. Samuel relaxed and released the breath he'd been holding as he caught sight of Margret approaching from the southeast. Despite the warmth of the late-June day, she wore an oversized cloak, which probably belonged to her father, over her shoulders and head, concealing everything and casting her face into shadows.

As soon as they stood about two feet apart, Margret leaned close enough for him to see more of her face and kept her voice low.

"Did you travel by way of the road and successfully locate the break in the trees?" She cast a glance to the left and right as if looking for someone who might have followed her.

"Yes. It was just as you described. I commend you on the accuracy of your instructions." He grinned, attempting to relieve her of the tension etched in every feature. "Am I to assume that you have used this rendezvous point before?"

Her head snapped up, and her eyes widened like those of a deer that knew it was about to become a hunter's prize. Samuel hadn't meant to alarm her or suggest that her actions were anything less than honorable, but he could tell by the look in her eyes that she believed as much.

He raised a hand to stay her worry. "Miss Scott, I am not calling your virtue or honor into question. I was merely trying to make light of the situation; however, it appears my jesting has not been well received."

Margret peered into his eyes, seeming to weigh him against some invisible scale, the measurement method remaining concealed. Finally she softened her expression and offered the hint of a smile.

"Forgive me, Mr. Lowe. You might be quite adept at maintaining your respected status among two differing sides, but Mama and Papa might change their mind about our friendship should anything appear improper. I am attempting to be as careful as possible to avoid suspicion."

"Yes." He nodded. "And I apologize for anything in my words that might lead you to believe I perceive you as anything less than the true lady you are." Samuel gestured toward the iron bench with its elaborate design along the top and sides. "Shall we sit?"

Margret positioned herself on one end of the bench, her posture ramrod straight. She reached up and pushed back the hood of her cloak, revealing hair that had been pulled back and fastened in an intricate arrangement of combs. He had grown so accustomed to the lappet cap she normally wore that seeing her hair unbraided and styled came as a surprise.

"Is there something wrong, Mr. Lowe?"

Her voice interrupted his silent observance, and he brought

his attention to her face. A mixture of amusement and uncertainty could be seen in her light brown eyes.

"N–no," he stammered. "Nothing at all, Miss Scott. I was merely taking note of the attractive styling of your hair. Forgive me for staring."

Margret reached up one hand to lightly touch the crown of her head. "Mama helped me this morning after chores. We have an engagement this evening in town at one of the homes along Water Street. She admonished me to take extreme care in whatever I do today so as not to ruin it in any way."

"An engagement on Water Street?" Along that street lived the most influential families of New Castle. "Is it to be a small affair?"

"From what I could determine, yes." Margret nodded. "As the evening is being hosted by the speaker of the assembly and his family, only those who have attained some level of authority within the assembly have been invited."

"And how is it that you are also included?"

Margret ducked her head as a tinge of pink stained her cheeks. "Mama and Papa thought it might be wise for me to socialize with any young men who might be in attendance."

She said nothing more, but the tone in her voice and the way she avoided his gaze said more than words ever could. If he calculated correctly, she would be approaching her sixteenth birthday near summer's end. The graceful way she had matured in the less than two years they had known each other was quite obvious to him. He only prayed the young gentlemen tonight would not see the gem he had found in Margret.

"How I wish I could appear at your door tonight and escort you to this affair." She looked up in eagerness at his words. "Alas, I have been summoned back to camp a little to the north this evening, and I must make my way there almost immediately after we part ways."

The initial zeal was replaced by a sad acceptance of the rather sobering reality of their respective duties. Were it another time or another place, Samuel wouldn't hesitate to ask permission to escort her this evening. There *was* the matter of her parents' approval, of course, but he felt confident he could sway them if given the chance. For now, he had to bide his time and pray.

"I am certain, Miss Scott, that you will outshine any other young ladies in attendance. And should the young men present not see your worth, may they be tarred and feathered for their lack of observation." He watched as she brightened with each word he spoke. "Of course, I would hope that amid the attention you will no doubt receive this evening, you will remember me and know how much I would rather be by your side than in the company of soldiers."

"Oh! I could never be happy with any other gentleman but you!" she replied in haste. "That is. . .well. . .I meant to say. . ."

Samuel had to hold his mirth in check at the way she floundered after making such a telling remark. She turned away from him, fidgeting with the strings that tied the cape at her neck. In the sudden silence, he could hear her shortened breaths. But despite the satisfaction he received from her confession, he couldn't allow her to remain embarrassed.

"Have you been discussing anything further with your father or uncle regarding the developments among the colonies?"

Margret leveled an appreciative glance in his direction and appeared to understand his tactic. She shifted on the bench to better face him and again found her voice. "Papa has observed my interest in political discussions and has made a point to include me as much as possible." She tapped a finger to her lips. "Most recently, he recounted the tale from Williamsburg a few months past about the lawyer named Patrick Henry, who became a member of the House of Burgesses last year."

Samuel nodded, knowing the man to whom she referred. "Ah yes. He stood before the house crowd and gave a speech that set the men on fire in favor of the patriot cause. His words appealed to people's emotions, and his passionate oration helped strengthen the resolve of the colonists gathered."

"Much like Thomas Paine's pamphlet *Common Sense*, published earlier this year."

"Exactly so." Samuel rested his arm along the back of the bench and crossed his ankle over his left knee. "These men have received the staunch support of those already convinced of the need for liberty, but they have made quite an impression on those who have not yet made up their minds."

Margret ran her fingers along the cords of her cloak. "Papa says the support of the colonists grows by the day, each addition making the men gathered in Philadelphia more and more resolute in their purpose."

"But not everyone in Philadelphia held the same perception of King George when they first assembled."

"Nor do they agree on how to proceed now, despite the majority being in favor of independence."

Margret had obviously spent a great deal of time educating herself during the months they were apart. Her arguments were clear and well supported, and her facts were in line with the information Samuel had been able to secure through his various connections on both sides. She possessed an intelligent mind as well as a seemingly dormant desire to play the part of an informant. He would be a fool not to take her into his confidence.

"Were you aware that Richard Henry Lee, one of the men serving as part of the congress in Philadelphia, proposed the idea of independence earlier this month?"

"No, I only know what I have heard from the men here in New Castle and what Papa, Uncle Edric, or Grandfather has shared with me after the assembly meetings."

"Do you not also spend time with the dressmaker in town?"

Margret inhaled a sharp breath. She placed one hand over her heart. "How do you know about my visits with Mrs. Thomason?"

Samuel had done it again. In his efforts to share with her what he knew and encourage her to do the same, he had instead caused an opposite reaction. With hands held out and a feeble shrug, he tried to appear nonchalant.

"I am a scout, remember? My duties require me to be fully informed about everything concerning the subject of my attention." He gave her a knowing grin to convey his true meaning. "I have a select network of informants who provide me with the information I need when I need it. They report to me on a wide variety of topics, and I trust them implicitly." Samuel reached for her left hand and covered it with his own. "Keep in mind, also, that I had to make certain of your alliances before I could proceed with our friendship."

That last line of explanation seemed to do the trick. Margret dropped her hand from her chest and offered a slow nod of acceptance. Good. He reluctantly released her hand and rested his own on his boot.

"Now, one more important development to note."

She raised one eyebrow and waited for him to continue.

"Following Mr. Lee's proposition, the congress was in a state of near pandemonium. Mr. Hancock had quite a time maintaining order in the room and convincing the men to settle down."

Margret scrunched her eyebrows and puckered her bottom lip. Samuel had to force himself to admire her eyes and not the appeal of her rose-colored lips.

"But if so many are in favor of independence, then why would there be such unrest among the men gathered?"

"For the mere reason that they all have different ideas about how to proceed with gaining that independence."

Understanding dawned. "So, since they cannot agree on a method to employ, they are in disagreement with each other and fighting amongst themselves, even though the outcome they desire is the same."

The way she summed up the entire dilemma impressed Samuel. Coming from her lips, the situation did appear to be foolish, but he doubted the men involved would feel the same.

"That is exactly right. If they do not find a way to come to an agreement, the British will continue their attacks against a somewhat divided Colonial army. And in that state, the superior British methods of fighting will end in a victory nearly every time."

Margret shifted and straightened her back. She tilted her head, as if pondering something of great importance, chewing on her bottom lip in a way that made Samuel want to lean forward and kiss her. As soon as the thought entered his mind, he shook his head, trying to dislodge the image. Margret had blossomed into a beautiful young woman, and he became more attracted to her with each encounter. But until his work was done, he was not free to pursue anything other than friendship. Where she was concerned, he had to keep that foremost in his mind.

"I see." Her voice forced him to pay attention to her words and not his errant thoughts. "So, what the men in Philadelphia need is someone to be brave enough to step up and say the words that it seems everyone is thinking. Right?"

"Uh. . .right." Samuel nodded, feeling like a fool. "Yes. That sounds like it might be the solution." He fought hard to get his brain working again, his attention back on the topic at hand and not on Margret's attractiveness. It wouldn't be a good idea for him to appear like an idiot after presenting his extensive knowledge just a few moments earlier. "But when you are dealing with men and their opinions on delicate subjects such as freedom, liberty, and independence, it is hard to gauge what the outcome might be even if they were to be incited into action."

She placed her hands in her lap and offered a demure smile, looking every bit the lady he knew her to be.

"Be that as it may, I am confident the men gathered will make the right decisions and that the fate of our colonies lies in good hands."

"On that point, I must agree." Samuel, himself, had done the research on the men who had been meeting on a daily basis in Philadelphia. Each colony had selected its best. But he did wish they could come to an agreement soon. They'd been meeting for more than a year.

"And now, I believe it is well beyond the time that I should depart. I have tarried long enough and must return to camp." He reached out and lightly clasped Margret's hands in his. "I do wish I could remain a bit longer, but we shall see each other again soon."

She smiled and rose from the bench. He had to force himself to maintain his resolve as he joined her.

"I do so enjoy our time together. Because of you, I have gained an appreciation for what is happening with the war against the British. Before we met, the primary concern in my life was the latest fabric that Mrs. Thomason had available in her shop or the newest shipment of goods arriving in port."

Samuel chuckled, knowing how true that statement was. He would have responded, had it not been for the serious expression on Margret's face.

"Thank you," she said with a soft sincerity.

Touching two fingers to his temple, he bowed slightly and dipped his head. "It has been my pleasure, I assure you."

As he started to leave, Margret touched his sleeve and he hesitated.

"Will you get word to me when you wish to meet again?"

The eagerness in her eyes made him want to stay, but if he did, he might do something he shouldn't and jeopardize their friendship. He'd also be late reporting to Major Johnson. After the excuses he'd given the last two times, he didn't want to be forced to provide a third.

"I promise, Miss Scott. You will not have to wait long."

She seemed to accept his answer, taking two steps back and putting distance between them.

"Very well, Mr. Lowe. Until we meet again. . ."

He watched as she turned and headed in the direction of Strattford House. Already he missed her. But he had a job to do, and he needed a clear head with which to do it. Despite his desires to the contrary, Margret Scott would have to wait.

❧

Margret stopped at the edge of the trees and took a few moments to compose herself. She smoothed the front of the cloak against her gown and took several deep breaths. Feeling in control again, she headed for the back of the house and did her best to appear as normal as possible. After wiping her hands in the folds of the cloak, she pushed back the hood, reached for the latch on the door, and slipped inside. She had almost made it into the enclosed stairwell that led upstairs to her room, when Mama's voice stopped her.

"Is this cloak to be a new addition to your wardrobe?"

With what she hoped was a contrite expression on her face, Margret turned to face her mother. Before she could answer the first question, Mama continued.

"Your brothers and sisters and I missed you during the mid-day meal. I trust your reason for not appearing is a good one?"

"Oh yes, Mama. It was." At least Margret believed so. "I

cannot tell you too much at this time, but I promise that you have no cause to worry."

She hoped there was no reason, anyway. The very fact that she had just met with Samuel unaccompanied was a definite concern.

"You are not engaging in anything that might compromise yourself or our family, are you?"

Margret hesitated. Mama should know her better than that. Then again, she *was* a mother. It was her duty to make certain her children were not doing anything that might besmirch their good name. And truthfully her association with a spy could bring harm to her family if she wasn't careful. Margret hadn't given that much thought until now.

"I see by your silence that you are uncertain." Mama folded her arms across her chest. "Tell me, does this have anything to do with the gentleman—Mr. Lowe, was it?—who has sent you two messages yet has not come to call?"

"He wants to call, Mama, but his duties make it impossible." Her mother wouldn't be appeased by that simple explanation, so she continued. "We have just met, yes, and I assure you he was nothing but a gentleman. Cousin Julianna has served as a chaperone once. She could verify what I say."

Margret didn't like the sound of pleading in her voice. She felt more like a young girl being reprimanded rather than a woman of almost sixteen. Mama seemed to sense her inner struggle and reached out to brush Margret's cheek.

"I only ask because I love you and do not wish any harm to come to you." Mama placed one hand on her hip. "However, I will not tolerate even the slightest indication that any of my children are acting outside of the realm of virtue and integrity."

Mama's words caused a small amount of guilt to creep into Margret's conscience. She slowly walked toward her mother and offered a reassuring smile.

"Mama, you have always been able to trust me. Although the circumstances are different this time, I promise that you can still trust me."

"Margret, my dear, I am not without my own secrets, or even the knowledge of the many ways I justified actions I knew were against the upbringing to which I was raised to adhere." Mama reached out and lightly clasped Margret's chin in her hand. "But I caution you to be certain that what you do is because you believe it is right."

The look in Mama's eyes said more than her words. Margret had heard the stories many times about how her mother had corresponded with Papa during the war with the French, and at the start, without Grandfather Gustaf or Grandmother Raelene even knowing. Even once they found out, Mama still refrained from admitting the full truth of the relationship she'd developed with Papa.

That was exactly where Margret was right now: torn between confessing to relieve the stress of having to be secretive and believing that if she admitted her feelings for Samuel, it would do more harm than good. Mama was sure to understand, but Margret wasn't ready to say anything. She worried the strings of the cape and chewed on her bottom lip. When Mama placed a hand on her shoulder, Margret stopped her fidgeting and looked up.

"If you say I can trust you, then I do. But promise me, when the time is right, you will come to me first? I do not wish to hear it from any of the ladies in our social circles who seem to take their very breath from spreading the details of others' lives to anyone who might listen."

Despite the earnest gaze Mama leveled at Margret, a second layer hid behind the first. It was one of a common bond. For the first time since she had met Samuel and agreed to their friendship, Margret felt as if she had someone else in her life who could relate to her situation. This came from the same woman who, at the age of fifteen, had hidden in the bushes outside of the town hall just to eavesdrop on an assembly meeting. And if she guessed correctly, Mama had let her see that second look intentionally. It was as if she was saying she knew the truth, but she was willing to let Margret confess on her own.

That alone lifted the heaviness in Margret's heart. Once again she turned toward the stairwell, but the front door opened and closed, interrupting her departure.

"I bring good news from town." Papa's voice boomed through the hall and echoed off the walls.

"Come to the back of the house, my dear," Mama called in reply.

Moments later Papa appeared in the doorway, almost filling the width and making the room feel smaller. His face brightened as he looked from Margret to his wife.

"Ah, my two favorite ladies."

Mama stepped forward and greeted him with a quick kiss to the cheek. When she stepped away, Papa regarded Margret, one eyebrow raised as a grin tugged at his lips. "And has my daughter become a cloaked marauder in my absence this day?"

"No, Papa." Margret giggled then mimicked Mama's greeting. "I went for a walk this morning to attend to a pressing matter." A question appeared in his eyes, and he looked to Mama. Her reassuring nod erased the curiosity. . .for now. "After the painstaking fashioning of my hair in preparation for the engagement this evening, the cloak merely protected the combs."

Papa tilted his head to the left and right as he observed Margret's coiffure. "I could see that something was different, but I could not determine it for certain." He pressed his lips together and nodded. "Beautiful." Sadness overtook his expression. "It is difficult for me to see that you are becoming a young woman before my eyes. Before long, you shall marry and begin a new life all on your own. And I shall have to bear the thought of not seeing my eldest daughter quite so often."

Margret wrapped her arms around her father in a hug and leaned her cheek against his chest, the rough wool scratching her skin. "Papa, you know I shall not go far. I could not bear to be away from you for that long." She pulled back and looked up into her father's down-turned face. "Besides, we do not even know who my future husband will be. If he has a desire to oversee this farm, perhaps we shall remain here, as you and Mama did with Grandfather Gustaf and Grandmother Raelene."

Papa brushed an errant strand of hair back and tucked it behind her ear. "Now that would be something to please me greatly."

"If the two of you are finished lamenting the potentially gloomy future that awaits, I would like to hear the news from town."

Mama tried to sound like she was scolding, but the soft light in her eyes betrayed her. Margret knew that she and Papa held a special place in Mama's heart. It was why they could usually get away with more than most in her family— and why even now, Mama came to her aid in not requiring an explanation. . .yet.

"Very well," Papa began and walked farther into the room. "I was at the port today in Wilmington when a small boat arrived, bringing news from Philadelphia."

He paused and scratched his chin, then he walked toward the window that overlooked the rear fields behind the house.

"Do not stop there, Papa." Margret came up behind him

and tugged on the back of his waistcoat. "Tell us the rest. What news came from the north?"

Papa turned around, a big grin on his face. The excitement in his eyes was almost contagious. "A man by the name of Richard Henry Lee proposed the idea of independence to the delegates gathered, and. . ." he drew out the continuation, "they are moving forward with plans to put it to a vote once all sides have been presented."

Mama clapped her hands together as a smile bigger than Papa's cracked her lips. The two of them shared in the joy, all but forgetting that Margret remained in the room.

"Do you not fear the consequences should the vote be in favor of independence?"

Her parents both turned toward her with raised eyebrows.

"It is certain that England will not favor such a proposal. With their forces far outnumbering our own, do you not hold any trepidation for what is to come?"

Papa stepped forward and stood directly in front of her. He tipped up her chin and offered a soft smile. "My dear Margret, you know we should hold no fear for the future, as God Almighty holds us in the palm of His hand." His face took on a more serious expression. "But you do make a valid point. And it is something the delegates at the congress are no doubt taking into consideration." With pursed lips, he regarded her curiously. "And where, may I ask, have you had the opportunity to ponder or discuss such specifics as these?"

Margret searched her mind for a suitable answer. "On several occasions, Papa. Do not forget that I spend time in town visiting with Mrs. Thomason and others. My friend Mr. Lowe is also quite informed. It is through those conversations that I have begun to assemble my own understanding."

Her answer seemed to appease him, and Margret inwardly relaxed. She joined her parents in rejoicing at the news, even though she had already celebrated when Samuel had informed her of Mr. Lee's proposal. But what would it mean for the colonies if they all voted in favor of it? What would happen in the war with the British? Life as they knew it was sure to change, and she wasn't sure they were ready.

seven

Margret stepped out of the candle shop, once owned by her great-grandparents, and stumbled as a young lad ran down the sidewalk in front of her. Wetness seeped into her shoulder where she leaned against the lamppost near the shop. She watched his progress as he rushed across the puddle-filled cobblestone street toward the town hall, only to stop at the top of the steps and shield his eyes as he looked toward the southwest side of town.

She followed the direction of his attentive watch but saw nothing. Did he think someone was coming? Had he heard from someone about something important about to happen? Despite having her doubts, Margret stepped onto the sidewalk and waited.

Nothing happened.

Confused by the boy's strange behavior, Margret decided to ask him about it. She lifted the hem of her skirts enough to avoid the mud and puddles from last night's thunderstorm and made her way across the street. The fresh smell in the air assailed her nose, and she breathed in the heady scent. Although she preferred the rains of spring with their sense of renewal, something about the summer rains struck a chord in her as well. It was as if God Almighty decided the earth needed cleansing and sent the refreshment to both purify and cool. And at the speed the young lad ran, the cool air did him well. He certainly would have fallen ill from his exertions had the normal heat of a July day been present.

As she drew closer to the town hall, she noticed the boy had his eyes closed. He also looked quite familiar. She ascended the steps and had almost reached the top when he opened his eyes and turned.

"Eli!" Margret exclaimed.

What was her cousin doing out here by himself? And where was Uncle Edric?

"Cousin Margret." Eli appeared to be startled to see her, as well. "I. . .I was just. . .I was just coming here for a few minutes before returning home."

He looked adorable when he was nervous. Margret didn't have the heart to scold him or order him back home just yet.

"And what is so important you had to run through town just to come up to these stairs and look toward the other end of town at nothing?"

"But it *was* something!"

The certainty in his voice surprised Margret. She looked again only to see the same thing she'd seen the first time. An empty street lined with several houses and a handful of shops, taverns, and restaurants. She turned back to face Eli, almost laughing at the determined pout of his lips and the fire in his eyes.

"Very well, then, how about you tell me what you saw? I would like to enjoy this sight with you."

"I was watching for the man on a horse who rode through town during a thunderstorm six nights ago on his way to Philadelphia."

Six nights ago? How did Eli expect to see something that had already happened? Her cousin looked well enough, but talk about seeing things that weren't there concerned her.

"Eli, you had your eyes closed. How did you expect to see anything?"

He gave her a look that made her feel like the daft one. Amazing how a nine-year-old boy could achieve that kind of reaction with just a glance.

"I did not need to see with my eyes, Cousin Margret. I saw with my mind."

"So you were imagining it, then." That seemed plausible. She reached for his hand. "Come, let us return to your home, and you can tell me as we walk. Your mama might take a switch to your backside if she discovers you were here alone."

Eli didn't argue. He seemed eager to do as she bade, allowing her to lead him down the steps and onto the sidewalk toward Water Street.

"Yes. Papa told me this morning about a man who was here. Someone important, but I do not remember his name. He said the man got a letter and had to ride to Philadelphia for a big decision."

A big decision. The vote for independence crossed her mind. It was the biggest thing that had been happening in this area for weeks. But why would someone ride all night in the rain? And why did he come from the south instead of from right here in New Castle? Margret had many questions, and she hoped Uncle Edric was at home to answer them.

"Why are *you* here, Cousin Margret?"

She looked down at Eli and smiled, still holding tight to his hand as they neared the river and the street that ran parallel to it. "I came to sell some candles and scented soap and to visit with Mrs. Thomason at the dress shop." And to meet with Samuel.

Eli didn't comment further. He simply walked alongside Margret and swung his arms back and forth. If they didn't reach his home soon, he might knock her arm out of its socket. She held him in check, though, while still allowing him his childhood fun.

"Here we are!"

Margret looked up at the three-story home with its newly

painted shutters on every window and the small covered porch that flanked the front door. Because of her uncle's involvement in the assembly, he had chosen a home in town where he could be closer to the events as they happened, rather than journeying the several miles from Strattford House. That pleased Mama, as she loved the farm. So when Uncle Edric announced his plans, everyone was happy. And he had selected a beautiful home, even if the one where he had lived before was much larger.

Three stone steps led from the sidewalk to the house, and the beautiful array of flowers gave testament to a well-cared-for home. She wondered if Aunt Sarah had done the work or if she had some of her servants do it.

Uncle Edric had said he fell in love with Aunt Sarah because of the beautiful gardening she did and the bouquets she delivered to the restaurants, taverns, and shops in town, as well as to the town hall in preparation for meetings when they were in session. That was how they had met, and as with her mother's story, Margret never tired of hearing it.

Eli knocked two times and waited for the servant to answer the door. Living in town required them to lock their door at all times. No sooner had the door opened than Eli barreled inside.

"Eli Hanssen!"

Margret covered her mouth and laughed at Aunt Sarah's voice traveling all the way outside. She remembered her own dash into her house nearly two years ago when she had first learned of the secret meeting Papa would attend. How times changed and yet stayed the same!

The servant held open the door for Margret then closed it. Since she had no wrap to remove, she simply nodded her thanks and proceeded to the rear of the house, where she was likely to find Aunt Sarah and Uncle Edric.

"Margret, my dear!" Aunt Sarah was the first to see her. "I did not know you had accompanied our Eli home. He had yet to get around to informing us of that fact." She leveled a scolding glare at her son, who shrugged and offered a sheepish grin.

Eli reminded Margret so much of her uncle, especially from the stories of the mischievous acts in which he and Mama had engaged. No wonder Grandfather Gustaf had considered the twins a handful. She could only imagine what she would do with two at a time.

"So, tell me, my dear." Aunt Sarah's voice broke into her musings. "Did you find our Eli out running around, or was he close by?"

Margret caught Eli's pleading expression and carefully formed her answer. "Papa drove Cousin Julianna and me to town this morning with specific tasks to accomplish. She left to attend to hers, and I encountered Eli on my walk. He was so excited, he ran inside, but it appears as if he forgot to tell you."

"That does sound like Eli." Uncle Edric's voice preceded him into the conservatory from his study.

Aunt Sarah looked up as he entered, and Margret took that opportunity to wink at Eli, who grinned in return. She understood what it was like to be a child and have fun. She also knew the importance of keeping a secret. Eli hadn't meant any harm, and if he hadn't been there, she might not have found out about this man on a horse during the thunderstorm.

"Good afternoon, Uncle Edric." Margret stepped toward him and placed a kiss on his cheek. If Aunt Sarah hadn't been kneeling in front of several potted plants, she might have done the same for her.

"And to what do we owe the pleasure of this visit from my favorite niece?"

"Oh, Uncle Edric, you are teasing again."

He laughed. "Yes, but I must pay high compliments to any

family member who enters my home. Otherwise, you might not return."

Margret smiled. "I shall remember that upon the next visit."

Uncle Edric came farther into the room and found a clear place to lean against one of the stone basins Aunt Sarah had ordered from New York for her garden not long ago.

"So, tell us, my dear, what brings you to our home?"

"In the brief encounter I had with Eli, I learned of a man riding through town six nights ago. Since he did not recall the specific details such as the name or the reason—but he did inform me that you told him about it—I came to inquire about the rest of the story."

"Ah yes." Uncle Edric pushed away from the basin, excitement spilling from every part of his face. "The news stirred everyone here in town."

"Who was it?"

"Caesar Rodney."

"The lawyer and delegate who had been sent to Philadelphia?"

Uncle Edric nodded. "One and the same."

"But I thought he was already in Philadelphia. Why was he riding through New Castle in the middle of the night?"

Eli plopped in the middle of the floor amid all of Aunt Sarah's flowers, his full attention on his father. Although he had no doubt heard the story already, he was eager to hear it again. Aunt Sarah continued to work, and Margret perched on a bench near the wall, awaiting Uncle Edric's reply.

"Are you aware of the proceedings taking place in Philadelphia as we speak?"

"Do you refer to the vote for independence spurred by Mr. Lee's proposal last month?"

Pleasure showed on Uncle Edric's face. "Just like your mother and grandmother before you. They both stayed informed about political developments."

"I admit that two years ago I was not so interested. But as time wore on, I wanted to know more." She didn't broach the subject of Samuel. For now, her parents' knowing was enough.

"Very good. Now, back to Rodney. He was in Dover attending to Loyalist activity in Sussex County when he received word from Thomas McKean that he and George Read were deadlocked on the vote for independence."

"Do you mean to say that one of those men did not want independence?"

"Yes, and that man was George Read, but it was more because he feared the consequences than that he did not want the liberty the vote would bring. He had expressed his concern over losing even more rights should the colonies make the separation official."

"So Mr. Rodney knew his help was needed?"

"Exactly." Uncle Edric nodded. "To break that deadlock, Rodney rode eighty miles through a thunderstorm on the first night of July, bursting through the doors in Legislative Hall." Chuckling, he added, "Still wearing his boots and spurs. He was just in time for the voting, so he cast his in with McKean, thereby causing the three lower counties to join eleven other colonies also voting in favor of independence. Now he has been elected as the Speaker of the House of Representatives here in New Castle."

Margret could understand why Eli had gotten so excited. She wished she could have been here to see it happen. At least she had the opportunity to hear about it soon afterward.

"What is even better," Uncle Edric continued, "is that immediately following that vote, which passed Richard Henry Lee's resolution, a man by the name of Thomas Jefferson from Virginia was nominated to draft an official document including all of the concerns and declarations of the delegates in the congress. He worked on it day and night for two days and produced the first draft just three days ago."

"What is it called?"

"The Declaration of Independence."

Uncle Edric said the name with such reverence that Margret couldn't help but be impressed. The very name invoked feelings of awe and wonder, but like George Read had expressed, it also produced uncertainty and fear.

"So, what will happen now?"

"Now, I believe they will review the words Mr. Jefferson penned and suggest changes until everyone is satisfied that the document contains everything necessary to adequately convey their feelings on this subject." He looked over at his wife and shared a smile with her. "Once the document is approved, every man present will sign his name to it. From there, it will be sent to England and King George."

The king of England. Margret could hardly fathom it. To think that a group of men from right here in these colonies had come together in accord, believing that life under the thumb of British rule was too much to bear. They had finally reached their limit, and now the king would know of it. She could only imagine the thoughts going through the minds of the men in Philadelphia. They would soon sign their names to a document stating that they were breaking free from all British control and establishing a form of self-government.

The king would be livid.

Margret would be petrified of doing such a thing. At least as a woman, she wasn't in much danger of her name being placed on a list of revolutionaries. But what about Uncle Edric and Papa and Grandfather? And the other men in the assembly? They were every bit as involved as the delegates in Philadelphia. Would they be in equal trouble?

"What vexes you, dear?"

It was Aunt Sarah's voice. Margret shook herself from

her thoughts and listened to her aunt and uncle. Both wore expressions of concern. When she looked around the room, she noticed that Eli was no longer with them. When had he left?

"I only worry about what will happen now. King George is not going to be pleased with this. And some of his army is already here, fighting against our militia."

Uncle Edric came and placed a comforting hand on her shoulder. "It is true that we do not know what we will face as a result of this declaration. But this time has not come by chance. We have fought long and hard for our rights, only to be brushed aside and taxed on an even greater level." He bent slightly at the knees so he looked Margret directly in the eyes. His compassion offered a modicum of assurance. "Much like the three lower counties separated from Pennsylvania because we wanted to govern ourselves, so do the colonies together wish to do the same, free from England's tyranny."

"But we separated from a colony much like ourselves and are seeking to become a colony of our own. We did not break free from a ruling power that has attacked us with brutal force. And what about the people who already live here in the colonies? Some do not wish to break away from England. Does this mean we will end up fighting against each other? Brothers in the same family, or cousins, or a father and son could disagree on this issue."

Margret knew she was rambling, but despite the joyous occasion this time should be, reality struck a hard blow. Not even the thought of seeing Samuel once she departed from her uncle's home brought relief from her worry.

It must have shown on her face, for Aunt Sarah rose from her knees to join Uncle Edric. She wiped her soiled hands on her apron and reached out to embrace Margret.

"My dear, many questions are to be asked at a time like

this. But, one thing we must remember and never forget." Aunt Sarah pulled back and tipped up Margret's chin. "God Almighty is watching over us. He knows everything that is happening and everything that will happen. He would not have allowed us to come this far if He did not have a greater plan in mind than what we can foresee."

She reached up and brushed a lone tear from Margret's face, a tear that Margret hadn't even felt. Obviously, this situation had her more troubled than she thought. But her aunt was right. They couldn't allow fear to stop them from doing what they felt was necessary. They were all in one accord, and they were moving forward, whatever the cost. Margret had to admire their bravery. She wasn't sure she would stand up against such a formidable opponent, but she knew in her heart that she agreed with all of them.

With another quick hug from both her aunt and uncle, Margret stepped back and composed herself. "Thank you both. What you say is true. We must not lose our faith or our hope. God Almighty has placed His hand of protection upon us. He has been with us this far, and I know He will not leave when we need Him most."

"You are quite welcome, my dear," Aunt Sarah replied.

"Now, I believe you should be on your way. I want to know that you arrived home before the sun begins to set." Uncle Edric gave her a parental look, one she knew well. "Do you have someone to escort you?"

"Yes," she answered truthfully, grateful they didn't ask for a name. Papa had asked her and Julianna the same question, and they had assured him a walk would do them both good. In truth, she hoped Samuel would offer to be their escort.

"It was good of you to stop by for a visit." Aunt Sarah placed an arm around Margret's shoulders in a loving squeeze. "You know you are welcome whenever you come to town.

Be sure to give our love to your parents and the rest of your family."

Margret nodded, hugging them both in turn. "I will. Thank you again. Good-bye."

Once the door closed behind her, she joined Julianna, who agreed to act as a chaperone, then she made her way to the riverfront and stood against a thick willow near the water's edge. She stared out at the river in front of her. It flowed day and night, never stopping, even when storms came and stirred the waters or a drought befell them and the height of the river dropped. No matter what happened, it pressed on toward its destination.

That was exactly what the colonists were doing. They were determined to succeed with their plans, and they weren't going to let anything get in their way. It also reminded her of Samuel and his conviction that what he was doing was right and what he was called to do. So many knew what they wanted and how to go about it. She wished she could claim that much confidence.

eight

Samuel walked along the water's edge and searched for any sign of Margret. As he neared a tall willow with its branches dipping low to the ground, he spotted her standing partially concealed within its shade. Her cousin perched on a large rock just to the south. Careful not to alert Margret to his presence, he approached until he was close enough that she would hear him.

"I suppose you have heard about Mr. Rodney's ride?"

Margret gasped and whipped around. "Mr. Lowe!"

She had once again selected the lappet cap and traditional gown that most young women her age wore, her hair again in braids. He wasn't sure if he didn't prefer her in the cloak. It lent an air of mystery that he found appealing. Still, even in everyday clothing, she was beautiful.

"My apologies, Miss Scott, for startling you." He grinned. "It does appear to be a habit I am developing."

She relaxed and offered a smile of her own. "I am to blame as well for becoming lost in a daydream."

"Oh? And what might cause you to become so lost in thought?"

With a nod toward the river, she sighed. "I was thinking about the perseverance of the river, then about so many people I know and how they hold such strong convictions regarding their purpose and their destiny. It caused me to ponder my own life." She turned pain-filled eyes toward him. "I realized that I do not know for certain what my purpose is."

Sympathy for Margret filled him. Taking one step closer, he

gave her a direct look.

"Miss Scott, although I know now that what I do is using my talents to the best of my abilities and aiding a cause in which I strongly believe, it was not always this way."

Her eyes widened, and her eyebrows rose. Good. She needed to know he could relate to her struggle.

"Just a few years ago, I had a similar conversation with my father. After growing up hearing the stories of how he had fought long and hard against the French and Indians, believing he was doing what was best for his wife and children, me included, I began to question my own desires and wishes for the future." Samuel glanced out over the wide expanse of the river as that conversation came back to him in vivid detail. "Rather than chastise me because I had not yet determined the course my life would take, he sat me down and grew quite serious. He told me that each man must decide for himself the path he will walk. No one can make it for him. But one thing that must be considered is how much you are willing to risk in order to accomplish what you set out to do."

He turned to face Margret again, taking note of the pensive look in her eyes. She was weighing his words carefully, and he could see the battle that raged inside. He wanted more than anything to offer her comfort or reassurance, but it wasn't his place to give. Instead, he reached for her right hand and held it between both of his.

"Miss Scott, you have already achieved a great amount of success in what you have learned on your own regarding the state of unrest among the colonies. You have also been a significant help to me, although you might not know it." He smiled. "So do not underestimate your contributions. Whether you have defined your true purpose or not, you have much about which to be proud."

Samuel raised her hand to his lips and placed a kiss on the back. His gaze never left hers, and he silently watched as first appreciation then tenderness filled her eyes. He was drawn to her, and their secluded location seemed ideal. As much as he wanted to declare the feelings simmering just under the surface, it wouldn't do either one of them any good right now. He needed to distance himself, so he released Margret's hand and took a step back. Yes, that helped.

"Now, as I allow you time in which to ponder those thoughts, might I return to my original question?"

Margret seemed surprised by the abrupt shift in the conversation, but she recovered quickly and nodded.

"I assume that with the ties your family maintains with the assembly, you have heard of Mr. Rodney's ride to Philadelphia?"

"Yes. And I have only recently left my uncle's house, where we discussed the event and the resulting consequences that might occur." Margret turned her back to the river, tugging on a long bough from the willow and regarding him with a sideways glance. "This Declaration of Independence will be sent to King George." She broke off a thin branch and started plucking the leaves by the stems. "Once that happens, I fear the situation here between the Colonial army, militia, and patriots and the British Army will escalate to far greater levels."

"Your assessment is no doubt correct. It is as I mentioned when you and I first became acquainted. The king will not take lightly a group of colonies refusing to cooperate. He is certain to dispatch even more troops and work twice as hard to assure a victory over the Colonial army here."

She looked over her shoulder at him, the worry forming deep brown pools in her eyes. "And that will bring the king's tyranny raining down on our heads in a thunderstorm."

"There are tyrannical acts being committed on both sides," he began in soothing voice. "I do not like to see anyone force his hand of control or rule as a dictator. I also do not like bloodshed of any kind, but sometimes it is necessary. I make it a point to do what I can to help assure a quick resolution to the conflict, and I serve where I am needed most."

Margret shrugged and resumed her original stance against the bark of the willow. Despair poured from every facet of her being. He simply could not resist any longer. Two steps put him directly behind her. He placed his hands on her shoulders, offering comfort. With a tearful exclamation, she turned and buried her face against his chest. Samuel held his hands out from her for a brief moment, surprised at this sudden turn of events, before wrapping his arms around her back and holding her close. He knew they shouldn't be embracing in this manner, but what was he to do? He couldn't exactly push her away in her time of need.

Choked sobs vibrated against his coat, and he tightened his hold. How good it felt to have her in his arms. She seemed to fit perfectly, the soft contours of her womanly shape pressing against him, a reminder that she was no longer a little girl. She clutched a fistful of his shirt just above the top button of his waistcoat as her weeping began to abate. He inhaled a healthy gulp of fresh air. If he didn't take charge soon, they would both be in trouble.

Gently, Samuel released his hold and put a few inches between them. With his thumb and forefinger, he tipped her face upward, then he reached into his pocket for a handkerchief to tenderly wipe the tears from her cheeks. She sniffed and offered a hesitant smile. The pouty shape of her lips drew his eyes to that part of her face. For a brief moment, he wondered what her lips would feel like against his. Just as he lowered his head toward her, she stiffened and backed away.

"Oh!" Margret pressed a gloved hand to the very mouth he'd almost kissed, her eyes wide as she stared at him. "I must have forgotten myself. I—" She paused and dropped her hand, both arms hanging at her sides as her chin jutted upward. "Forgive me, Mr. Lowe."

Her composure impressed him, but he couldn't allow her to take all the blame. "The fault is mine, Miss Scott." Samuel extended his hands, palms up. "Do accept my apology for my attempt to take advantage of you in your present state. I only meant to offer comfort. It was improper of me to assume anything more."

She nodded but didn't offer further words. It was up to him to get them back on track, and he prayed he could manage the difficult task. With a glance at the waning sun overhead, he found his topic.

"If you are to be certain to arrive home in time for supper, you should head that way now." At her crestfallen expression, he crooked his arm. "Might I be permitted to escort you? I know of a team of horses we can use." He must remember to thank Thomas for that.

Without hesitation, Margret placed her hand at the bend of his elbow and allowed him to lead the way. As they passed her, he caught Julianna sending Margret a questioning glance. Relief crossed her face at Margret's nod, and then she fell in step behind them as they walked toward the carriage.

The majority of the ride toward Strattford House took place in comfortable silence. After what had almost happened by the river, they both needed that time to collect their thoughts. As they reached the turn off the main road, Samuel pulled the carriage off to the side and hopped down from the seat. He turned to offer his hand to first Julianna and then Margret.

"I apologize that I cannot deliver you both to the front

door, but I fear if I tarry much longer, I shall again be late reporting to my commanding officer."

Julianna was the first to speak. "We appreciate your escort, Mr. Lowe." She cast a teasing grin toward Margret. "And I am certain my cousin is happy to continue alone, as explaining your presence might prove a challenge." She placed a hand on Margret's shoulder and regarded them both. "Now, I believe I shall depart for my own home and leave the two of you to say your farewells."

Samuel almost protested. Leaving them alone might not be the best decision, but at the controlled emotion in Margret's eyes, he remained silent, offering only a nod as Julianna walked away.

"I meant to inquire earlier," he began, seeking a neutral topic. "Have you and your uncle or your father discussed any of the battles that have taken place thus far?"

She tilted her head and chewed on her bottom lip, a quirk he had come to find endearing.

"We did talk briefly about Boston when the British left that city earlier this year. Papa also talked about the fighting that took place around the Canadian border, as that was where he spent a lot of time during the war with the French." She cast a quick glance in his direction. "And I believe there was mention of movement closer to New York as well as farther to the south in the Carolina colonies."

The fact that her father shared so much made him even more confident about their continued relationship. If her father trusted Margret with details such as those, then he no doubt impressed upon her the importance of being careful. And that meant Margret would take the same caution in regard to any questions that might arise about him.

Samuel crossed his arms and leaned back against the carriage. "I must admit that I have come to enjoy being able to discuss all of this with you. Not only does it give us a common topic in our conversations"—he paused and grinned—"but it provides me with a bona fide reason to continue our meetings."

Margret turned up one corner of her mouth in a smirk. A teasing twinkle entered her eyes. "I am pleased to hear that you do not wish to end our friendship, Mr. Lowe. After all," she added with a shrug, "what reason would I have to venture out were it not for your desire to rendezvous with me?"

The charming manner in which she delivered the coquettish remark made Samuel wish to close the distance between them and show her just how much he wished to continue their relationship. But that had almost gotten him into trouble earlier. Once again, propriety ruled, and he reined in his thoughts. One day soon, though, he hoped for the opportunity to be more honest.

"Miss Scott, you do make the necessity of my leaving a difficult order to follow. And as much as I would like to tarry longer with you, my duties require that I be elsewhere."

It took a moment for the meaning behind his words to dawn on Margret, but once they did, a becoming blush stained her cheeks. She reached up to tuck an errant curl behind her ear as she dipped her chin closer to her chest.

"I shall do my best to get word to you again soon about the time and place of our next point of contact."

Margret nodded. "Very well, Mr. Lowe." She extended her gloved hand toward him. "Until such time as we see each other again. . ."

Samuel took her hand in his and bowed to place a kiss there. As he climbed back onto the high seat, he called down to her. "Remember not to allow your uncertainties about your purpose to cloud your vision about the contributions you already make. Trust in God Almighty to show you the way."

With one final glance in her direction to make an imprint of her face on his mind, he snapped the reins and set the horses in motion, turning them toward the northeast and heading for the British camp.

❧

Several weeks later, Margret recalled every detail of that conversation and time together, including the way the breeze from the river had stirred the few locks around Samuel's forehead, begging her to reach out and brush them back. She couldn't remember ever being so attracted to someone, nor feeling such a strong desire to encourage his advances. Gratefulness still filled her that they had put a stop to their near kiss that day. Over the past few months, a handful of young men—mostly the sons of assembly members—had done their best to gain her favor. One or two were quite dashing, but Margret's mind kept returning to the memory of Samuel's face. Every other young man paled in comparison.

Although Mama had wanted to invite some of the young men to the celebration of Margret's upcoming sixteenth birthday, news of the thirty thousand British troops landing in New York in mid-August cast a shadow over the festivities. The Declaration of Independence had been signed, and just as Margret predicted, King George had not been happy. He immediately dispatched more soldiers from his army to join a large contingent of troops already present in the colonies. From the moment they set foot on land, they attacked and conquered, securing a string of victories from Long Island and New York City all the way to Lake Champlain.

So, instead of greeting the young men at a celebration, Margret ended up bidding them good-bye as they left their families to join the ranks of the Colonial army in fighting the British. Some men even turned their backs on their families as they remained in staunch support of the British and refused to fight for the Colonial army. A time that should have been joyous ended up being shrouded in fear and anguish. New York was only a little over one hundred miles from New Castle. If the British continued their advance, it wouldn't be long before they would march on Pennsylvania and then the three lower counties.

The only welcome news through all of this came in the form of an excited announcement from Uncle Edric in late September. Margret thought he would break their front door the way he came bursting through the entrance.

"We did it! We finally did it. We have succeeded in all of our attempts, and now it has finally happened."

Once the entire family had gathered in the front hall, Papa broke the stunned silence caused by Uncle Edric's disruptive entrance.

"What happened, Edric? What or who has gained a great success?"

Uncle Edric paused for a moment to catch his breath, then he beamed a smile at everyone. "The three lower counties. We now have a name all our own."

A name! Their counties had a name. Margret could hardly believe it. She could see the excitement written on everybody's face, and though she wanted badly to ask the question she knew everyone was thinking, it was Papa's place to do that.

"Did they make the choice we thought they would?"

"Yes." Uncle Edric nodded. "We are hereby no longer known as the three lower counties. From this day forward, we are and shall forevermore be Delaware."

"Delaware?" The word burst forth from Abigail's lips.

Papa looked down at his youngest daughter with a smile, patted her lappet cap, then returned his attention to those gathered. "We have taken the name from a gentleman by the name of Sir Thomas West, or Lord De La Warr, a governor of

Virginia. He explored this region before heading farther south to take up residence there, and as we desired to form our own identity, his name provided the best inspiration."

Delaware! To think they now had their own name! They had become an official colony in their own right, not just a continued extension of Pennsylvania, despite their separation earlier that year.

"We have adopted our own constitution, and. . . ." Papa paused and looked at each member of the family in turn, excitement shining in his eyes. "Which town do you believe they have selected as the one that shall serve as our capital?"

"New Castle!" Nicholas burst out with the answer.

"Exactly right." Uncle Edric clapped his nephew on the shoulder and stepped back, his bearing straight and pride emanating from every facet of him. "There has even been discussion about who will serve as our first president, with John McKinly earning the majority of the favorable vote. Nothing official has been decided yet, but the tide does appear to be turning in that direction."

"When shall we know for certain?" Margret could no longer contain her excitement. And her curiosity had gotten the better of her.

"The exact time is unknown," Uncle Edric said, "but from all appearances, it seems we shall have reached a decision no later than one month hence. George Read was the president of the Constitutional Convention here in Delaware that led to the adoption of our governing document and the selection of our name. He demonstrated admirable leadership skills, and with Caesar Rodney as Speaker of the House, I do not believe it shall take them long to reach a decision."

Mama reached down to pull Abigail closer, and the little girl snuggled against Mama's skirts. "Mayor McKinly has served this area well during his time as mayor of Wilmington.

I see no reason why he would not make a fine president of newly established Delaware."

Papa and Uncle Edric both nodded, but it was Uncle Edric who spoke. "Most of us in the assembly agree. George Read was also a consideration, but he stepped out, saying he was content with his current position with the assembly."

"And with the uncertainty regarding the British advance or occupation," Papa added, "we must be prepared for an attack very close to home. Establishing our government and setting a plan in motion will aid us in maintaining the independence we have so long desired."

Silence settled over everyone as they processed the bitter truth behind Papa's statement. Although most would rather pretend the threat of British invasion did not exist, the reality was that the chances remained quite high. The Delaware River controlled access to the ports in Philadelphia. Up to now, the patriot ships and blockades had managed to keep the British at bay, preventing any attempt to access the river as a way of reaching what the British considered to be the center of the Colonial rebellion.

Even if the British decided to come via the Chesapeake Bay, New Castle County still presented a barrier. They would have to march across land and pass through Delaware to reach Philadelphia.

Margret hadn't realized just how important their little colony was. William Penn had no doubt known that when he had claimed the rights to the three counties that now made up Delaware. As a colony, though, they had even more freedom to act as they deemed appropriate, instead of being left to the mercy of Pennsylvania's dictates. If only they could get Kent and Sussex counties to agree as well. Margret had been shocked to learn that many to the south of New Castle still felt their lives would be better if they remained under

British rule and protection.

More than ever, Margret wanted to see Samuel again. Not only did she wish to share this great news with him, but she also enjoyed learning so many other details that her father and uncle neglected to share with her. Or if they did, she learned of the events after they had already become part of the past. At seemingly every turn, Samuel was becoming an even greater part of her life—a fact that didn't bother her in the least.

&

October came and went, and with it, so did the end of the harvest season. Margret thrilled at the wide variety of vegetables and fruits that once again overflowed from every surface in the kitchen. Their cellar would be quite full this winter. They might even be able to provide their excess to the soldiers who had joined with the Delaware Regulars to fight.

As they moved toward the end of November and then approached Christmas, a somber mood settled over their house and most of the region. Reports had been arriving almost weekly announcing victory after victory for the British. Margret didn't understand how the Colonial army could continue to withstand the onslaught and still come out fighting. Each time she met with Samuel, the length of his visits shortened. It was clear his duties required much more of him.

The redcoats marched across most of New York and had even begun to advance in New Jersey after capturing Fort Lee. With each passing day, fear of the war coming almost to their front door became more prevalent. Even the normal joys of Christmas were supplanted by the southern march of the British. General Washington's army had suffered many crushing losses. The men were ill, malnourished, and had lost much of their resolve. But from the letters sent by

Washington to the congress in Philadelphia, he did everything he could to keep his own spirits high.

Two days after Christmas, Margret secured the thick, woolen cape around her shoulders and head and went outside to gather a few twigs for the fireplaces inside. Most often the servants performed this chore, but Margret insisted upon doing it today. Mama hadn't argued.

As Margret gathered suitable branches and twigs, she wondered if she would see Samuel before the year's end. Then as if her thoughts had conjured him into reality, there he stood directly in front of her, his handsome face wrapped in a wool scarf and his smile warming her from the inside out.

Although she wanted to shout out his name, someone would hear, so instead, she returned his smile and nodded for him to follow her to a more secluded location. As with the other visits, a pang of conscience struck her at the impropriety, but Samuel had been nothing but a gentleman in her presence. She didn't expect him to be any different today. Once they had reached an area deeper in the grove of trees to the west of the house, Margret took a moment to observe him more closely. Despite the obvious happiness he displayed at seeing her, sadness reflected in his eyes as well.

"What is it?" she asked.

Samuel bent down and picked up several sticks, then he stepped close and placed them in her arms. He sighed. "I have received a summons to accompany my regiment south of here into Virginia."

So he was leaving again. That meant this visit would be the shortest of them all. She forced a brightness she didn't feel into her voice. "When do you leave?"

"Two days hence."

"But why now? We have heard about the battles and victories to the north. What interest is there in the south?"

"Many influential men are in Williamsburg. And with the recent victory of General Washington at Trenton, the British are attempting to employ another tactic."

Margret shook her head. "A victory? For General Washington?"

Samuel regarded her with confusion. "Had you not heard?"

"No."

"General Washington rallied his troops on Christmas night and took them across the Delaware River north of Philadelphia. The Hessian troops in Trenton had celebrated the holiday a bit too much and were surprised in their drunken state by Washington's army in the early hours of the morning. Not even an hour later, the battle ended, and nearly nine hundred prisoners were taken captive. Washington is now headed toward Princeton in hopes of capturing that town as well."

Finally! After all these months, the Colonial army needed this.

"I assume this victory went far toward boosting the morale of Washington's men?"

Samuel nodded. "A great deal so, yes. It also provided them the opportunity to gain some much-needed guns and ammunition." He paused and seemed to consider his words carefully before continuing. "But now, the British have been driven north again. So, they have devised another plan of attack. That is why I must go."

Samuel obviously thrilled at the announcement of General Washington's victorious attack. Despite his pretend allegiance to his British regiment, his true loyalties shone clear and bright.

Margret startled when Samuel reached out and touched her cheek. It was the first time since that encounter in July when he'd been so bold as to initiate such tender contact.

"I do not know when I shall return or how long my regiment will remain in Virginia. But I do promise that as soon as is possible, I shall come back to you and perhaps discuss the future in greater detail."

She could see the inner battle that raged in his eyes. His words held so much more meaning, but she knew he was not at liberty to share anything more. A burning sensation developed just behind her eyes. She fought back the tears that threatened to form and instead put on a brave face. It would not be fair to Samuel for this last sight of her to be one of sadness.

Hugging her armful of kindling, she lifted her chin. "I pray God's protection over you, no matter what you may face. And if it be His will, I pray you return soon to me."

Samuel started to step closer but stopped. He swallowed several times and formed his mouth into a thin line. Margret understood exactly how he felt, for she fought her own battle.

With nothing more than touching two fingers to the tip of his three-corner hat, Samuel turned and departed, leaving Margret with only the memory of his face to comfort her.

nine

Thoughts of Samuel were all that kept Margret warm throughout the winter months. Even once the spring thaw came and preparations were made to begin the planting season again, she couldn't seem to muster enough enthusiasm to enjoy the annual airing of the house as she had in the past. Papa had hired more workers outside, and an additional servant inside the house increased their productivity. That didn't quell the need for a distraction of some sort to take her mind from Samuel, though. Even her visits into town had lessened. With the blockade of the ports and the nonexistence of any goods being imported, traveling to town didn't excite her as it used to.

Mama had noticed her change of demeanor, but not a word was said. Margret caught the concerned glances every once in a while, and she fought almost daily with the desire to confess everything. She had promised Mama the truth when the time was right, but that time wasn't now.

The distraction she needed came in the form of a letter from her cousin in Williamsburg. Papa's brother had moved there when demand for his skill in working with leather produced an invitation from another saddler in town. At first, he had provided the British with some of the finest saddles in the colonies, but as the unrest between the British and colonists grew, he limited his work to those who were against British rule.

Margret took the letter and rushed upstairs to her room. She and Hannah had exchanged letters for years before the war began, but since that time, no word had been sent. Three years older, Hannah often offered insight and wisdom that Margret yearned to gain as well. Eager to learn how others were faring during the tumultuous times, Margret broke the seal and began to read:

Dear Margret,

How I have missed our regular correspondence since the day Governor Dunmore ordered the removal of the gunpowder barrels from the magazine nearly two years past. The weeks and months have been difficult to bear without word from you. Not long after the angry protest of our town's citizens, Governor Dunmore sought refuge on a British warship in the York River. The thought that the British remained so close has made living here in town an exercise of caution and alarm. . . .

Margret well understood that type of life. Thus far, they had been spared the presence of the British other than the occasional soldier who visited New Castle in the early months of the war. But now, the British stayed far enough away that Margret had at times been able to pretend the war wasn't happening. She continued reading her letter:

I do not like living as if our entire lives are at risk. So many of the men and women have been heralded for their bravery, and had it not been for the sage counsel of Mr. Peyton Randolph, I do not believe our town would have been able to maintain the calm it has achieved for the past two years. Even Papa has seen a decline in requests for his fine saddles and workmanship with leather. Because of the increase in the cost of goods, not many citizens are able to afford more than the basics to survive. . . .

The cost of goods had risen in New Castle as well. As much as Margret would have liked to purchase a new gown, Papa could not afford it. Thankfully, they had the farm to provide all of their food, but frivolities had been denied. She couldn't begin to fathom what might have happened had her family owned a shop in town like Hannah's father. Papa had seen the cost of iron materials increase, but thankfully they had been able to find what they needed right here in the colonies. As she read, she was even more grateful for their home and the reassurance that came with it:

> *Although we have succeeded in keeping the British from overtaking the town, their influence is still very much alive. Life as we once knew it has ended, and it has been replaced by a life that is foreign to us all. Old friendships have been strained and families divided. Former loyalties to the crown are questioned and new ones to the patriot cause have been demanded. It has made my heart sad to see brothers fighting against each other and sons rejecting the guidance of their fathers because they believe in the independence the Colonial army is fighting to achieve...*

Margret thought about the young men who had bidden her farewell on their way north to fight. She recalled both the anger and the sadness on the faces of the family members who parted ways in disagreement. So many felt so strongly about one aspect or another, and they all allowed these feelings to divide them. Margret prayed that one day they might find reconciliation. She didn't like to see such pain, and it appeared to be prevalent throughout the colonies.

> *Soldiers and militiamen have taken up positions through-out the town. While their presence is comforting in some*

ways, the sight of so many is a daily reminder that we are at war. Tongues must be guarded, and even the slightest hint of poor commitment to the rebellion has been enough to punish the guilty party. A man by the name of Joshua Hardcastle consumed a bit too much in a tavern one day and uttered some rather inappropriate remarks. As a result, he was dragged from the tavern into the streets and brought before a mock court-martial. They threatened to give him a coat of thickset for his betraying words. Men had the hot tar and the feathers ready, and they had even stripped off his shirt in preparation.

Oh, Margret. I do not know if similar circumstances are taking place up north where you are, but if they are, I pray that you and everyone remain safe. . .

Tar and feathers? Margret shuddered. Not only did this Mr. Hardcastle suffer humiliation in public by being dragged into the town streets, but the fear that he might actually have to be subjected to that type of punishment must have been terrible. No, nothing like that had happened here in New Castle, but she had no doubt similar situations took place in Boston, Philadelphia, or New York.

Despite all of this, I do have some good news to share. In May of last year, the Fifth Virginia Convention met at the capitol building here in town. The result of that meeting was to declare the entire colony of Virginia independent. We are now a commonwealth. They also approved a declaration of rights and a state constitution. Then in late July, amid military parades, the discharge of cannons, and the firing of small arms, the Declaration of Independence was proclaimed to the cheers of everyone all over town. Celebration and joy continued well into the evening, and we saw a beautiful

*display of fireworks that illuminated the town. Papa said
many toasts were given and drunk by revelers at the Eagle
Tavern, but he did not divulge any further details. . .*

Margret smiled at this. Samuel had told her of some of the
drunken states of the soldiers in his regiment after a victory.
Given the level of excitement surrounding the unanimous
vote in favor of independence, she could easily imagine
the spectacle some men would create amid their toasts and
revelry.

But fireworks! Even though there had been rejoicing in
town as the news from Philadelphia reached them near the
end of July last year, they had not been fortunate enough to
witness a display of colorful explosions such as that. What a
sight it must have been!

*I understand from reliable reports that your colony has been
fortunate enough to undergo a similar liberation. Delaware
is a fine name, and many citizens here love the fact that
you chose it after one of our governors. I must admit that
it sounds and looks better than the pretentious appearance
of Lord De La Warr's name. But with these individual
declarations added to that of the colonies as a whole, I fear it
will anger the British even more. Since our establishment as
a commonwealth, we have settled into a routine, but one that
is still tenuous in regard to the war. The economy is declining,
and there has been talk from the new General Assembly of
moving the capital to Richmond. Many Tidewater councillors
in the Upper House are against it, but their influence is waning by the day. Should the British threat become serious, I can
see the wisdom in moving the capital further inland. But if
that does occur, I shall miss residing in the center of so many
new developments. . .*

Margret took a moment to think about the possibility that the same might happen to New Castle. Like Williamsburg, it had been established as the capital because of its convenient location to water and easy access to many of the major roads or waterways connecting them to other important towns. But should a British attack ensue, their town would become a viable location for the British to make their headquarters. She prayed it wouldn't happen, but she couldn't deny that it might. Where they could move the capital to avoid that, she didn't know.

But do forgive me for slipping once more into less-than-pleasant thoughts. I want to also share some more good news with you. After nearly two years of courting, John Carter has finally asked Papa for permission to marry me, and Papa agreed. We are to be married in October of this year. I cannot begin to tell you how excited I am. Mama is, too. We will not have the grand ceremony that Mama and Papa wanted for me, but I am happy enough knowing that I will soon become John's wife. He is a cabinetmaker in town, with a trade already established. So I know that once this war is behind us, we shall recover from the losses and be well on our way toward achieving even greater success.

And now I must conclude this letter, for I fear it has already become much longer than you might have time to read. There has been so much to share with you, and as I do not know when I shall be able to write again, I wanted to address it all. I hope this letter reaches you in a timely manner. It has been a wonderful exercise to write to you again.

With love,
Hannah

Margret read through the letter one more time before folding it and rushing from her room downstairs to the kitchen, where Mama was preparing dinner. Nicholas and Andrew were near the barn, working on a wagon wheel, and Papa hadn't yet come home from the shipyard. She stepped around Lydia and Abigail, who were playing a game with marbles on the floor near the doorway. Her youngest brother, Micah, stood near Mama, attempting to put his finger in the pudding sauce, but Mama smacked him with a wooden spoon. He pouted and held his hand close to his body, but he didn't try a second time.

"I have a letter from Cousin Hannah in Williamsburg!" Margret waved the sheets of paper high in the air as Mama turned from the counter.

"It has been some time since you have heard from her. What does she say?"

"She will be married later this year!"

Joy transformed Mama's face. "Oh my! That is exciting. Does she say anything about the ceremony they have planned?"

"They do not have much at the moment, so the wedding will not be as grand as they had hoped, but she is happy nonetheless."

"What is this I hear about a wedding?" Papa opened the door at the rear of the house and stomped his boots against the iron block before stepping inside. "Is someone getting married?"

Margret ran up to her father and gave him a quick kiss on the cheek. "It is Cousin Hannah, Papa. I received a letter today from her."

Papa's eyebrows rose, and he looked over Margret's shoulder to where Mama stood wiping her hands on her apron. "And what else does my brother's daughter have to say?"

Margret consulted the letter again and repeated the general idea of the details Hannah had provided. When she looked up, concern was etched in the faces of both her parents.

"It appears that we could be facing the British head-to-head after all," Papa remarked to no one in particular.

"How nice it was to hear from Hannah," Mama agreed, "but what she shared in her letter, I believe, shall serve as a warning to us to take precaution in the coming months."

They continued to discuss specific parts of Hannah's letter throughout the evening meal and how things might change in New Castle, but Margret's thoughts had drifted toward a handsome soldier who was down in Virginia at that moment with a regiment that may very well be making plans to march on New Castle.

&

Two months later, and one year after the colonies had declared their independence, Margret received another letter. This one was from Samuel. In it, he shared how he preferred her company to that of the uncivilized behavior of some of the soldiers and that he longed for the day when his duties would once again bring him north to her.

Margret took the letter and returned to the stone bench where they had met on more than one occasion. She pored over each and every word, savoring the expression of Samuel's feelings and receiving comfort from the brief note. When she reached the end, though, she was surprised to read about the plans of a British fleet carrying General William Howe's army toward Head of Elk to enter by way of the Chesapeake in August. She didn't believe Samuel should be sharing details such as this with her, and she wondered at his purpose.

Recalling the worry on her parents' faces after reading Cousin Hannah's letter not too long ago, Margret was torn. She didn't know if she should reveal these details to Papa or keep them to herself. If she said something, would they ask how she knew? Admitting the depth of her relationship with

Samuel remained difficult. Although she could read between the lines of his letter and know that his feelings for her ran as strong as hers did for him, she could not bring herself to confess that to her family just yet.

But what did Samuel expect of her? What exactly did he want her to do?

ten

Unable to determine a plan of action in response to Samuel's information, Margret continued her normal activities, each day wondering if that would be the day the British would invade their town. As Samuel had stated in his letter, near the end of August, the British fleet landed at Head of Elk and prepared for their march to the east as part of a campaign to capture Philadelphia. A flurry of activity ensued in New Castle and among the assembly, as well as in the House of Representatives. Margret walked along the back part of the house on her way to the far stairwell and heard voices coming from behind the partially closed door of Papa's study. Curious, she approached the door and did her best not to step on any of the floorboards that might creak.

"I do not like what I see and hear, Madison."

Margret didn't recognize the voice as any she had heard in recent months. She tried to peer through the crack in the door, but the man remained hidden from view.

"Thanks to the report we have received from a young man serving as a spy in the British camps nearby, we know they are not long from here."

A Colonial spy? Margret couldn't help but think of Samuel and wonder if he was the informant or if he was somehow involved with passing that information along.

"Yes, it is a matter of great concern." Papa's serious voice held a note of foreboding.

"I have already spoken with President McKinly and Caesar Rodney, as well as McKean and Read. Your brother-in-law, too, has given his approval. Now I wish to run the details by you, as it will involve the use of some of your ships."

"Proceed."

Margret held her hand in front of her mouth to conceal the sharp intake of breath as she realized she was eavesdropping on a battle plan by the soldiers and willing militia in the area. Papa's visitor spoke of the action they would take should the British pass through New Castle and make their way toward Wilmington. With both towns so close to the water and Papa's ships anchored not too far from the river's banks, the man in Papa's study asked him to be prepared to fire on the British from the river. They would not expect it, nor would they be able to escape the attack other than to run in the opposite direction from where they were headed.

"I believe this tactic shall thwart their advances and perhaps give our armies a chance to rally against them."

"But what if the British do not pass through our town and instead march a little farther to the north and west, closer to the Pennsylvania boundary?" This was Papa asking the question. "What good will firing from my ships do then?"

"To be honest, Madison, I had not thought of that possibility. It seemed logical that they would want to take control of the towns along the way rather than avoid them."

Margret saw movement through the crack in the door, and she stepped to the side to avoid being seen. Straining her neck forward, though, she could glimpse Papa's profile as he spoke with the man opposite him.

"And that may very well be the case, William, but we must have an alternative measure of defense in place should the British do as I suggested they might."

"I shall take this under consideration and present the possibility to Rodney tomorrow. As the Delaware militia is his to command, he will no doubt take all precautions against an attack, no matter where it originates."

Papa folded his arms across his chest. "My brother-in-law has informed me as well that General Washington is moving in this direction from more remote areas of Pennsylvania. The Colonial army he commands intends to meet the British halfway and do everything within its power to stop their progress toward Philadelphia."

"And I have heard that General Cornwallis and General Howe are not men you wish to encounter on the battlefield."

"That may be true," Papa countered, "but General Washington is every bit as formidable. He would not have lasted this long as commander in chief of the Colonial army if his skills had not kept him alive."

"There is to be a meeting at Aiken's Tavern tonight where more details shall be discussed. Can we count on you to be in attendance? It will give us more facts to present to Rodney upon the morrow."

"I will be there."

Margret straightened when it sounded like the meeting was coming to a close. She sneaked away from the door as fast as she could and rushed outside. While she tried to catch her breath, the pounding of horse hooves on the dirt made her look up to see a rider approaching.

The young courier stopped directly in front of her.

"Miss Scott?"

"Yes?" How did this young man know her name?

"I have a note for you."

She reached up and took the folded piece of paper and opened her mouth to ask who sent it, but the lad immediately turned his horse and kicked it into a gallop as they sped away.

Margret watched their departure for several moments before looking down at the piece of paper in her hand. With care she broke the wax seal at the edge and unfolded the note:

I am camped with a regiment at the head of the Elk River. Meet me behind the Harland farm barn after dusk. I will be waiting.

That was all the note said. She recognized Samuel's familiar scrawl, but why would he send it to her now? She had longed to see Samuel for many months, and now she finally would. How would she steal away unnoticed? The Harland farm was only three miles from the western edge of her family's land and just past the boundary line into Maryland. But what about the safety of a young woman traveling alone, not to mention a young woman who aligned herself with the patriots going to meet a man presently camping with the British?

The idea of sneaking under the cover of semidarkness to meet with Samuel thrilled her, but the fact that she might be discovered didn't. He would no doubt be wearing his officer's uniform, and should anyone see her consorting with a redcoat, it could put an end to her relationship with Samuel. She prayed he had taken every precaution. Now it was up to her to do the same. Samuel wasn't the type of man to expect anything less, and his faith in her abilities gave her courage. He knew the dangers involved, and he would most likely rather see himself hanged than place her in a position of discomfort.

Armed with that assurance, Margret set about making plans to escape right after dinner. Papa would be joining many others at Aiken's Tavern, and Mama would be busy putting the younger children to bed. She knew she could succeed.

⁂

After shifting her weight from one foot to the other for what felt like the hundredth time, Margret pushed away from the back of the barn and squinted to peer into the darkness. No rustling of the trees in front of her, no branches snapping beneath the weight of a person or horse, and no evidence that anyone else was nearby. Nothing interrupted the still of the evening except the early sounds of creatures coming awake for their nocturnal activities.

Had she misread Samuel's note? To reassure herself, Margret reached into her pocket for the brief message only to find it missing. No! She was certain she had tucked it beneath her gown and petticoats before she left. It couldn't have fallen out. So where was it?

Frantically, Margret searched her memory in painstaking detail. No matter how hard she tried, she couldn't recall where Samuel's message might be. Oh how she hoped no one else had come upon it, or this evening might end more quickly than she had planned. But for the moment, she had another concern—Samuel's absence. She prayed he hadn't encountered any problems with getting away to see her or anything worse.

Unsure whether she should continue to wait or start toward Elk Landing, Margret prayed the good Lord would show her the path to take. The only answer she heard was the recall of a verse from the proverbs in the Bible—one Mama had insisted she memorize at a young age and keep close to her heart: "*In all thy ways acknowledge him, and he shall direct thy paths.*"

Margret turned her face toward the ever-darkening sky, marveling at the number of stars that lit the inky canvas she observed. "Lord, I am in need of Thy guidance. Thou hast promised to direct my path. I must place my trust only in You. Tonight I require that guidance more than ever. Please lead me in the right direction."

Comforted by both the verse and her prayer, Margret mounted her horse, adjusted her clothing, took hold of the reins, and headed west. Elk Landing was another seven miles. With every step, she prayed Samuel would approach from behind or to the side and prevent her from traveling all the way to the camp. She clutched the cloak tighter around her body and pulled the hood down over her face as she stayed just within the tree line, her path lit only by the almost full moon above.

At the edge of one set of trees, she heard the faint rumble of voices not too far ahead of her. She couldn't have gone that far, so who else would be out in the middle of nowhere? Was Samuel bringing someone with him? Carefully, Margret dismounted and crept toward the sound, stopping when she saw two British soldiers gathering wood, neither one of them in any way resembling Samuel. She held her breath and took a step backward when her horse sidestepped and released a rather loud puff of air.

The snort shattered the near silence, and the two soldiers whipped around to stare in her general direction. One dropped his armload and reached for his pistol. The click as he cocked the hammer reverberated through the clearing. Margret held her breath.

"Who goes there?" one man hollered into the darkness.

Frozen in place, she could only stare out from what she hoped was a secure spot and pray they didn't investigate. Her heart pounded so loud she was sure they could hear it, and her breathing came in short gasps, like droplets of water sizzling and jumping in a hot frying pan.

Where was Samuel?

"I see you have managed to put the enemy on full alert, my dear," a soft voice said from just behind her left shoulder.

Margret covered her mouth and swallowed the scream at Samuel's sudden appearance. The two soldiers in front of them remained poised as they peered into the trees but had yet to make a move.

"Do allow me to see to these gentlemen," Samuel whispered. He stood and placed one finger over his lips before slowly venturing out from the protection of the forest. "Hold your fire, Richard, it is Samuel Lowe."

The man waited until Samuel approached before returning his pistol to its holster. By the time Samuel reached the two men, they were too far away for Margret to make out what any of them said. She watched as the soldier with the pistol gestured wildly with his arms and the one still holding an armload of wood shook his head. Beyond that she couldn't make out facial expressions or anything else about the conversation taking place.

In a matter of moments, it was over, and the two soldiers headed in the direction of where Margret assumed their camp to be. As soon as they disappeared from sight, Margret inhaled a deep breath and released it. That was too close. A few seconds more, and she would have been discovered and kidnapped—or worse. But she didn't want to dwell on that.

Samuel, too, waited until the soldiers were gone before turning toward her and closing the distance between them. He spoke as he walked.

"Do you have a keen desire to put your entire life in danger, or did your eagerness to see me cloud your good judgment?"

The scolding tone of his voice gave Margret pause, but the moment he was close enough, she jumped at him and threw her arms around his neck, more grateful than anything to see him.

"Had I known this was the type of reception I would receive," he said as he held her tight, "I would have allowed those two men to take you prisoner so that I might be your rescuer."

Margret jerked back and gasped. She heard the teasing in his voice, but it didn't offer any comfort. How could he jest about something like that?

Immediate remorse crossed his face, and he placed his hands on her upper arms. "Forgive me, my dear. I do not wish to make light of such a dangerous situation." Consternation replaced the remorse as he stared down at her. "But I would like to know why you did not wait for me at the barn."

"I waited for almost an hour! Fearing something dreadful had happened to you or believing you had been delayed, I decided to walk a ways in your direction."

"Did the thought of the dangers of being detected not cross your mind?"

"Yes, but I did not intend to go far." Despite her initial certainty that she had made the right decision, in light of what had almost happened, her explanations sounded shallow.

"Well, it is fortunate that I came upon you when I did."

He looked at Margret and gave her a questioning look when he took note of the breeches she wore beneath the cape. His perusal turned to admiration as his gaze lingered, and Margret felt the warmth of embarrassment creep up her neck. She couldn't exactly do what she did tonight hindered by layers of petticoats.

"Now, allow me to assess your choice of attire this evening. I must admit, it is rather charming. . .and pleasing."

Margret looked into his eyes, transfixed by the deep emotion she saw reflected there. Rather than allow her imagination to run away with her, she batted her eyelashes and dipped into a curtsy. "Why, thank you, my good sir. I fashioned it myself."

The chuckle that followed lightened the mood and soothed her apprehension. After completing his visual assessment of her wardrobe, he turned his attention to her face. He extended his arm and encouraged her to walk as he guided her and their horses back in the direction she had come. The early hoots of an owl blended with the chirps of crickets and croaking of frogs in a nearby pond. Although she loved nature in all of its symphony, she unconsciously stepped closer to Samuel.

In response, he tucked her hand into the crook of his elbow and covered it with his other hand. With a quick glance, he made a silent promise to her that he would keep her safe. But safety wasn't exactly the feeling that fought for control inside of her. Margret was grateful for the cover of darkness that hid the blush she felt burn her cheeks at her errant thoughts. She needed to stop thinking of Samuel that way.

"When do you intend to tell me the reason for the note you sent asking me to meet you?"

Samuel tilted his head and regarded her. "Is it not enough that I had a desire to see you? Must I have a reason?"

"To bring me out alone after dusk? Yes."

"I do confess to wanting to be with you." He lowered his voice and leaned down. "But there is a more pressing matter, which requires your assistance tonight."

His warm breath wafted across her cheek, and she shivered. Something about the combination of the secrecy with the fact that she was alone with Samuel at night gave her a heady sensation.

When Samuel didn't continue, Margret pulled back to look him full in the face. He stared at her for several moments as if he were trying to commit her image to memory. Finally, he stopped and took her hands in his.

"What I am about to tell you is of the utmost importance."

Margret nodded, not wanting to say anything that might cause Samuel to change his mind. But by the determined look in his eyes, she didn't have to worry about that.

"You are no doubt aware of some of the plans for that regiment now behind us, along with many others who are camped nearby, to proceed east and toward Philadelphia."

Again she only nodded.

"Their numbers are quite substantial, and with the leadership of two generals who have seen their fair share of victories, I believe they shall prevail. But with Caesar Rodney in charge of the Delaware militia, his thoughts on a plan of action need to get into the right hands, perhaps helping to even the odds a bit more on the colonists' side."

"Why are you telling me this?"

Samuel looked over her shoulder then back at her. "I have learned of General Washington's arrival at a tavern not far from here. I thought perhaps you might find a way to notify him of all that I have told you."

Margret gasped. Notify General Washington? She couldn't take critical information like that and flounce into a tavern, delivering a message to the commander in chief. What if someone in his camp found out what she had done? What if someone found out Samuel was the one who had told her? If she did what he asked, she would be perceived as a spy, and that was just like what—

Realization dawned on her.

She recalled the remark by the man who visited Papa, saying that a spy in the British camps had gotten word to them of the British arrival at Head of Elk.

"Mr. Lowe, are you—"

"I only want to do what is right, Miss Scott."

Margret saw the wisdom in his reluctance to give her a straight answer regarding the full scope of his duties. But she knew he was the man of whom her father's visitor spoke. He had told her almost from the start that he was a spy, but she didn't know a friendship with him would come to this. Each time they met, she had gotten more deeply involved. There was no turning back.

"Very well." She nodded. "I shall do as you request." Although she had no idea how.

Relief filled every part of his face, and he slipped a folded paper into her palm. "Thank you, Miss Scott. This means a great deal to me, and I believe it will mean a lot to General Washington."

If she *lived* long enough to see the results of her deceptive behavior.

"Now, I would like to escort you back home, as the sun has fully set, and I do not wish for you to ride back unaccompanied."

"I appreciate your thoughtfulness, Mr. Lowe."

He bowed, and Margret almost laughed at the formality they both enacted. She allowed him to help her mount, then she waited for him to do the same. Silence settled over the two of them as they reached the Harland farm, but Margret found comfort in it. The more distance that stretched between them and the British camp, the more secure she felt. She still didn't like having the British this close, but at least she had escaped detection by any of them.

Just as they crossed the border between Maryland and Delaware, another horse came out from the dense copse of trees to their right. Startled, they both reined in their mounts and stopped. When the moonlight hit the face of the rider, Margret gasped.

"Nicholas!"

eleven

"What are you doing here?"

Margret couldn't have been more surprised if Papa himself had appeared.

"I might ask *you* the same question." Nicholas looked from her to Samuel, distrust written all over his face. "So this is who sent that cryptic message to you."

The note! She *had* dropped it. Before she could ask how he found it, he continued. "Why are you associating with a British soldier? If Mama or Papa knew, they would—"

"Please, Nicholas." Margret urged her horse forward until she came alongside her brother's. She reached out and touched his arm. "I promise you that what you believe you are seeing is not what it appears."

He yanked his arm away and glared at Samuel, animosity and disapproval fairly shouting from his expression. "What I see is that you have crept away from the house without letting anyone know where you were going, only to ride three miles in order that you could engage in a secret rendezvous with this British soldier."

"His name is Samuel Lowe." Margret sent a pleading look in Samuel's direction, and he returned it with an apologetic one of his own.

"I do not care about his identity or the reasoning behind what you have done this night." Nicholas shifted his gaze away from Samuel and toward her. "Do you not realize the danger in which you have placed yourself?"

"But, Nicholas, that is what I am trying to tell you. There

was no danger." Unless, of course, she thought about the two soldiers in the clearing. But she wasn't about to tell her brother that. "Mr. Lowe is a man you can trust. I promise you. And if you would take a moment to allow me to explain, you would no doubt find that I am correct."

"You can explain on our way back home." Nicholas grabbed hold of her reins and sent another scathing glare at Samuel. "I shall see that my sister arrives safely."

Furious at how her younger brother was exerting authority over her, Margret yanked her reins free and urged her horse to take a few steps away from her brother.

"Mr. Lowe is perfectly capable of accompanying me, Nicholas. He is a perfect gentleman and has kept me from any harm."

"And I shall make certain it stays that way."

"But—"

Samuel cleared his throat. Margret and Nicholas both turned to face him.

"I believe it is best if I return to camp and leave the two of you to complete the journey by yourselves. My presence is the source of hostility, and I do not wish for members of the same family to engage in an argument because of me." He wrapped his reins around his wrist and nudged his horse in reverse. "Miss Scott, I do apologize for any problem I have caused you this night. Please forgive me, and remember what I said."

Margret wanted to stop him, but she knew it would only cause further trouble. "I will," she said as she watched him disappear into the night. Once she could no longer see him, she turned on her brother.

"What did you think you were doing, following me and intercepting us both when it was clear I was in no apparent danger? Do you realize that *you* could have been shot if you had caught Mr. Lowe off guard?"

If Nicholas had been younger, he might have cowered beneath her anger, but at fifteen, he was nearly a man. And by the look in his eyes, he was not about to allow his sister to speak to him that way. . .even if she *was* older.

He jammed his index finger into his chest and stared at her. "Me? I found that note you dropped and followed you so that I might see where you were going, only to find out you were paying a visit to a British soldier, and *you* are angry at *me* for what *I* have done?" He huffed. "I did what I did because I do not wish you to get hurt. You?" Nicholas jerked his thumb over his shoulder in the direction of where Samuel had just disappeared. "You did not consider what might happen should you be discovered or should Papa learn where you had gone."

Margret knew she would never get through to her brother if they remained angry at each other and allowed their emotions to get the better of them. So she took several calming breaths and tempered her ire. With one deep breath, she pressed forward.

"Nicholas, I am pleased that you care about me enough to follow me and see me safe from harm, but what you do not realize is that there are other, more important issues at hand than the destination of my journey or the identity of who I met there." He started to respond, but she held up a hand. "I cannot tell you everything about tonight, but please, all I ask is that you trust me when I say that I have done nothing wrong. And until the time is right, do not tell Papa about anything you have seen here tonight."

"You are asking me to speak a falsehood? What will I say when he asks us why we were out riding this late at night?" Nicholas folded his arms and jutted his chin into the air. "I will not lie to him."

"I do not expect you to lie, Nicholas. I only ask that you

not speak of this of your own volition. And do not worry," she reassured him, remembering that their father was at a tavern meeting tonight. "Papa will not know we were gone tonight."

Her brother remained silent for several moments, his mouth rigid and forming a tight line as his eyes narrowed. Margret shifted in her saddle. If she was going to still reach General Washington tonight, they had to get back to the house.

"Very well," he finally said. "I will trust you. . .this time." His tone held a note of warning. "But do not expect me to provide you with an alibi should this happen again."

Margret turned away and smiled. Her brother could be difficult, but she still had a way with him that would guarantee the success of her mission.

"Now, let us make our way home before we are gone any longer."

She pressed her heels into the horse's ribs and squeezed her legs, thankful that her brother hadn't mentioned anything about her not riding sidesaddle. Allowing Nicholas to remain at her side, she urged her horse into a gallop, and her brother's mount followed suit. In a matter of minutes, they were back on family land. Margret stopped them both as they reached the main lane leading to the house.

"I shall take the horses to the barn." She nodded at the house. "You can use the door on the south corner so that you enter on the side opposite from where Mama is."

Nicholas dismounted alongside her and handed her his reins but paused before leaving. "What about you? How will you explain coming inside from the barn at this late hour?"

If only he knew where she planned to go after he left. It would be even later when she returned from the tavern.

"I spend a lot of time there. Mama knows that. It will not appear unusual, and if she inquires, I will tell her that I needed some time to myself." At least that wouldn't be a complete lie.

She *would* need time to herself after she completed the task ahead of her.

Nicholas still didn't seem sure about the entire ordeal, but he accepted her reasoning and instruction and left her to make his way toward the far corner of the house.

Margret waited until she saw him disappear inside before walking both horses along the edge of the property in the direction of the barn. Once she had secured Nicholas's horse, she led hers out the rear door of the barn and mounted again. When she approached the break in the trees that lined the front edge of their property near the road, she sped her horse up to a gallop almost immediately. As its hooves pounded on the ground beneath them, echoes of Samuel's words hammered in her head.

British campaign. Philadelphia. Marching to the east. General Washington. Tavern. Head of Elk. Right. Wrong. Spy.

All of it swirled around in her mind as she closed the distance between her home and the tavern where she prayed she would find General Washington. It was the only tavern where she knew a meeting was taking place tonight. And Papa and Uncle Edric would be inside. What if they spotted her? Or what if she couldn't get to the commander in chief without a disturbance?

The glow of the lanterns on the poles outside the tavern showed two soldiers standing guard over the horses and the door. At least she knew she'd found the right place. Stopping just shy of the circle of light formed by the torches and lamplights, Margret dismounted and tied her horse to the nearest pole.

She pulled the hat from the satchel tied to the saddle and set it firmly on her head, pulling the brim down low and tucking every bit of her hair underneath it. With that done, she withdrew Samuel's note and held it out in front of her then did her best to walk with confidence toward the door to the tavern.

When she approached, the two soldiers stepped closer together and blocked her entrance. Margret cleared her throat to avoid sounding like a woman and kept her face purposefully turned away from them as she waved the folded paper in front of them but did not allow them to take it.

"I have a message for General Washington."

She hoped her voice was disguised enough to convince these men she was a lad and not a lady, but they didn't immediately step aside to let her enter. Frantically searching for something that might make them move, she tried again.

"It comes from a man by the name of Caesar Rodney and regards the British encampment at Head of Elk."

That worked. Without a word, one man reached for the latch and pushed open the heavy wooden door. Margret stepped inside, the smell of ale, rum, and tobacco immediately assailing her nose. She looked around the room. At every table, four or five soldiers sat with mugs in hand, some somber and some jovial, but all of them appeared to be enjoying themselves. A deer's head was mounted on the back wall farthest from the door, and a bearskin covered the wooden floor in front of the fireplace. Raucous discourse sounded from so many voices talking at once.

Her eyes scanned every nook and cranny until she finally saw Papa and her uncle in a far, dark corner, set apart from the main room by walls on three sides. They didn't even look up at her entrance, too engaged in whatever discussions were taking place at their table. Breathing a sigh of relief, she resumed her visual search and stepped into the middle of the din.

Margret didn't mind the noise, as it might cover her conversation with the general without raising too much suspicion. Searching each one of the tables, she finally spotted a man wearing a finely tailored uniform and a decorated cocked hat sitting on the table in front of him. That had to be the man she sought. Making her way as quickly as possible through the scattered tables, she weaved in and out of the men until she reached the table where General Washington sat. She stood in front of him.

He looked up when she approached, as did every soldier who sat with him. Had it not been for the stories she had heard of his personable nature, this man might have intimidated her. She was thankful he was sitting, as seeing his height in person might have caused her to flee. But she was here for a reason, and the sooner she accomplished it, the sooner she could leave.

"General Washington, sir?"

"May I help you?"

"I have a message for you, sir."

He extended his hand, and she almost lost her nerve. She couldn't afford the time to be timid, though. She had to deliver the message and make her exit. . .fast. With shaking hands, she passed the note to the commander and shifted from one foot to the other as he read. When he looked up from the note, he regarded her with a question in his eyes. Margret swallowed. What if he didn't believe her? What if he thought it was a lie, meant to deceive him and his armies? She held her breath as he looked at her in silence.

A moment later, appreciation appeared on the general's face. Obviously, he had determined what he needed to verify the contents of the message and the validity of her plight.

"Thank you. This has been most helpful. Please tell the man who gave you this information that I am in his debt."

Margret nodded, afraid of saying anything further for fear that they would discover her identity. Realizing she had done what she had come here to do, she turned to leave. A tug on the edge of her cape stopped her. When she looked over her shoulder, General Washington crooked his finger, indicating she lean down. She did.

The commander in chief drew close to her with an amused look on his face. "And the next time you deliver a message such as this, you might wish to return to your skirts and bonnets rather than breeches and a hat. I assure you, you will get much further with the men."

Margret felt the blood drain from her face. But when he sat back in his chair and gave her a wink, she relaxed. He had no intention of giving her away. With a nod of thanks, she headed for the door. As soon as she stepped outside and reached the spot where she had tied her horse, she nearly collapsed. She couldn't believe she had actually stood before General Washington and managed to speak, let alone deliver the message Samuel had given her to pass on to him. And she had again escaped notice. . .this time from two men who meant the world to her.

What a tale this would make to tell her children and grand-children one day. At that thought, Samuel's face once again popped into her mind. She mounted and pointed her horse toward home. With any luck, she could sneak into the house and upstairs without anyone else noticing she was gone.

twelve

Three days after he had ridden away from Margret and her brother, on the thirtieth of August, Samuel stood with the other soldiers in their regiments as they listened to General Howe and General Cornwallis give the orders for them to begin their march. Thankful that his regiment had been among the first to be called, Samuel secured a place in front where he could scout for them. When necessary, he could steal away unnoticed, just as he and Thomas had planned.

As they left the Elk River behind and headed east, he began to recognize some of his surroundings. They were just a mile or two north of the road that led to Margret's family farm and about fifteen miles west of the capital of Delaware. Curious why they didn't head toward New Castle, Samuel had asked some of the other soldiers the night before and learned that the plan was to avoid the two principal northern towns in Delaware as much as possible. General Howe didn't want to run the risk of encountering too much opposition from possible militia or soldiers in the Colonial army hiding in the houses and other buildings. No, he preferred the open space where he could meet his enemy head-to-head.

The only problem was that the Colonial militia and army didn't fight from the open fields on a consistent basis. They had at the beginning, but after several defeats, they began to fight in a manner familiar to them—using brush, hills, trees, and anything else that might give them the upper hand.

Samuel preceded the army as they crossed the border into Delaware and peered with a trained eye into the heavy brush that lined the road. He caught sight of movement to his left and looked again but saw nothing. A few hundred more feet, and something moved to his left. He was sure of it. This time, when he turned to look, Thomas signaled him from behind the concealment of the trees. So he *had* been right!

Samuel cast his gaze to the right and left, then to the rear. They were far enough back and around a bend, so they'd never see him. With as much care as possible, he dashed up the slight hill and into the trees to join Thomas and the other men lying in wait for the right moment.

He grabbed a rifle and silently told Thomas that he'd secure a spot ahead of the army where he could fully utilize his accuracy at a great distance. General Washington and Brigadier General William Maxwell had hand selected these one hundred men for this mission. One of the men near the front looked vaguely familiar to Samuel. With questions to the right soldiers, he learned the young man's name was Hanssen and he lived on the farm that neighbored Strattford House.

Of course! Samuel remembered one of the times he had met with Margret. Her cousin had been a chaperone, and she had introduced the young lady as Julianna Hanssen. So this young man must be related somehow. Having him there gave Samuel a sense of connection to Margret. But the thought that Mr. Hanssen might be killed in this exchange also crossed his mind. Of course Samuel knew he himself could be killed or injured, but it wouldn't be the first time that danger lurked close by. He took up a position just ahead of the Hanssen lad, determined to stick close to the young man and do everything he could to ensure his safety. What good were his skills at a distance if he couldn't pick off the soldiers who might fire upon the militia?

From his vantage point, he could see the prime placement of the light corps and how they had maximized their position to take full advantage of a surprise attack.

As soon as the signal was given, they opened fire.

Almighty God, be with us now.

The British rushed to present arms and take aim against the militia, but they couldn't tell the direction from which the shots were fired. Using tactics taught to them by the Indians, the special group set up a system of continual fire and forced the British to halt their progress east.

Samuel watched the men in his regiment, along with the rest of the British soldiers, plant themselves to make a stand against their enemy. He only prayed the Colonial militia had enough ammunition to last.

෨

Four days later, the fighting continued. The British had succeeded in making small advances each day, and on September third, the action came to a head just to the east of Cooch's Bridge. An open field spread out before them, and the two armies faced each other.

Samuel watched from his concealed location on the upper level of the barn that belonged to the house next to the field. He looked out over the outnumbered light corps and knew this didn't bode well. But one thing caught his eye. Near the front of the Colonial army, a man held a flag high above the soldiers. Next to him stood the drum and fife players, but it was the flag that held his attention.

He had seen a similar one flying above Prospect Hill in Boston, but this one was different. The red and white stripes looked the same, but in the top corner nearest the pole was a blue box with white stars arranged in a circle. From this distance, he couldn't tell how many, but if he made a guess, he'd say it was thirteen.

Samuel had to admit, the sight of that flag drove home everything that had become important to him during this struggle. No matter how often he faced the fear that they might not succeed at what they wanted to accomplish, he remembered their unity. Despite fighting against what appeared to be overwhelming odds, they were bound together by their shared desire for freedom and liberty.

Even today, as they faced an army that possessed more ammunition and greater numbers than they possessed, they still stood strong and fought with valor.

Lord, Thou hast been with us throughout this entire war. Continue to make Thy presence known and give these men strength, no matter the outcome.

As the volley of shots were fired from both sides and soldiers fell from within the ranks of both armies, Samuel knew history was being made. Almost immediately, it became evident that the light corps of the Colonial militia would not succeed. Many in the rear sounded out the retreat, while others engaged in hand-to-hand combat against the British troop offense.

At the end of the battle, Samuel once again walked the border between the two sides and was able to get a general assessment of the damages and the wounded. As near as he could determine, about thirty men from each side had given up their lives for the cause, while many more from the Colonial side had been captured and taken prisoner. Walking among the wounded and dead with the British soldiers, Samuel came upon the young man he had tried to protect throughout the battle. But he couldn't be in two places at once, so he had lost track of the lad.

He knew he had to act the part of a British soldier. Since General Howe had ordered all living men to be taken prisoner, Samuel checked for any sign of life in the man at his feet. He prayed for something. Otherwise, he'd feel like he had failed Margret as well.

The young man stirred and moaned. *Praise be to God Almighty!*

Samuel knelt down and tried to assess the wounds. The bleeding had stopped, but this man needed attention and soon. Samuel called for a stretcher and helped another soldier lift the man onto the makeshift bed.

"Jac. . .Jacob."

The words were barely discernible, so Samuel leaned close. "Please, do not try to talk. You are going to be safe."

"Jacob," he said, more clearly this time. "Jacob Hanssen."

So, that was his name. At least he would have something to share with Margret when he saw her next. He might not have been able to spare Jacob from injury, but he was determined to see that the young man made it safely home, no matter what the cost.

❧

For eight days, the British regrouped and prepared for their next attack. General Howe commandeered Aiken's Tavern in New Castle, while General Cornwallis used the Cooch House as his headquarters. Once they had regained their strength and added to their numbers from other regiments who joined them, they continued their march toward Philadelphia.

"If all goes well today, we should have a clear path toward the capital city."

Samuel held back the grunt of disdain at the man's elation regarding the defeat of the Colonial army. He had managed to conceal his true contempt for the British the entire time he was spying for the Colonial army. But in light of the recent defeat so close to Margret's home, he wasn't sure how much longer he could maintain this ruse. If he didn't rejoice with the other British, they would know something was amiss. But if he did celebrate, he felt like a betrayer. So, instead, he offered to take many of the watches over the prisoners.

Two days later, word reached him of the success at Brandywine. General Washington's eleven thousand troops were no match for the British force of nearly eighteen thousand. They had put forth a valiant effort but ended up having to retreat to Chester, leaving Philadelphia dangerously exposed.

"Gather your belongings and prepare the prisoners for travel."

Samuel sat upright at the booming sound of Major Johnson's voice. "Where are we taking them, sir?"

Johnson turned. "We have occupied Wilmington and will be using several locations in town where our wounded can recover and these prisoners can remain secure."

Samuel joined the other soldiers in following Johnson's orders. Throughout the entire ordeal, his thoughts were centered entirely on Margret. What must she and her family be feeling right now? Despite their best efforts, they had failed to stop the British campaign. Now they had lost not only many of their sons and fathers but their town of Wilmington, as well.

As they resettled the prisoners and established an order for the watch, Samuel made plans to visit Margret that evening. He didn't care what he had to do to make that happen. He only knew he must see her.

&a.

Waiting for the opportune moment, Samuel crouched low near the northwest side of the barn and watched the main house for any sign that Margret might come outside. She told him she often visited the barn after dinner to say good night to the animals before she herself retired. He prayed tonight would be one of those times.

After twenty minutes, light outlined the back door near the kitchen, and Samuel straightened, recognizing Margret's form as she approached the barn. He didn't want to startle her, but he had to return to Wilmington posthaste.

"Miss Scott," he called in a loud whisper.

Margret jumped at his voice and placed a hand on her chest. "Mr. Lowe?" She peered into the night, looking for him.

Samuel stepped into the light and reveled in the joy that lit up Margret's eyes when she saw him. Eagerness made her steps light and quick as she rushed to join him. But as soon as she stood before him, her expression changed and sadness crept in.

"Mr. Lowe, the situation is awful. We have suffered such loss."

He felt her pain and reached out to touch her cheek, offering what comfort he could. "I know, Miss Scott, but you must not give up hope. The British might have control of Wilmington, and they might even occupy Philadelphia, but do not underestimate General Washington's determination or that of your fellow colonists. The tide could change when you least expect it."

"Thank you, Mr. Lowe. I was in great need of hearing that this night." She offered a brave smile then drew her eyebrows together. "Was there a specific reason you came tonight? I know you must be quite occupied with your duties."

He appreciated the fact that she got right to the point. It would save him the possibility of offending her when he had to leave hurriedly.

"Yes, I came to provide you with an update on the British advancement toward Philadelphia. Now that they have defeated Washington at Brandywine, almost nothing stands in their way. Wilmington is being used as their present headquarters, but I am sure that will change once they occupy Philadelphia."

"And you? What are your duties now that the fighting has diminished for the present?"

Samuel debated telling her about Jacob in the house where he stood watch several times a day, but as he didn't have a plan established for bringing him home, he decided to save that for another time.

"I have been assigned to the prisoners captured from the battles of Cooch's Bridge and Brandywine. It affords me the opportunity to learn of critical battle plans while serving in a capacity that is of very low risk."

"I am pleased to hear that you have kept yourself free from most danger, Mr. Lowe. It would be quite difficult for me to bear any news that harm had befallen you."

Her heartfelt yet indirect admittance of her feelings for him bolstered him like nothing else could.

A door opened and closed near the house, and Samuel immediately slipped into the shadows, pulling Margret with him. He peered around her and didn't see anyone approaching, but they couldn't take any risks.

"I must return to Wilmington, Miss Scott." He reached for her hands and held them tight for the fleeting moments. "Please take what I have told you tonight and do with it what you are able. I will try to steal away to see you soon. While we are apart, take extra precaution to stay safe and remember to never lose your hope."

"I promise."

"Margret!" Her father's voice called from somewhere between the house and the barn.

Samuel had to leave. Now.

With a final look at Margret, he slipped farther into the darkness and made his way back to Wilmington. Their brief visit had only whetted his desire to be near her again, so as he rode back to town, he began forming a plan.

≈

Margret remained hidden as she watched Samuel go. Once she was sure he was safe, she slipped around the corner of the barn and into the doorway.

"Margret," Papa called again. "Are you out here?"

"I am here, Papa." Margret met her father at the bottom of

the slight hill leading to the barn. "Was there something you needed?"

He shook his head. "No, but with the British occupying Wilmington, I do not want you to spend a lot of time outside alone. It is not safe, and it would devastate me if anything should happen to you."

"Very well, Papa. Let me say good night to the horses, then we can close the doors and return to the house."

Together, they walked among the stalls on the lower level of the barn, speaking to each animal in turn as they made their way back to the entrance that faced the house. With the doors closed, Papa extended his arm, and Margret tucked her hand inside his elbow.

"Forgive me for sounding overly cautious, my daughter, but your welfare and safety are of the utmost importance to me. We have just received word that President McKinly was taken captive, along with our key documents and funds, which were secured in Wilmington."

"Oh, Papa, not President McKinly!"

"I am afraid so. With the British remaining so close, there is talk about moving the capital to protect it from further invasion."

"But Papa, the British are moving toward Philadelphia. And from there, they will most likely head back into New York. What need would they have of occupying New Castle?"

Her father stopped in his tracks and turned to face her. "Where did you hear of the British attack plan?"

Margret silently chastised herself. She hadn't thought before speaking, and now she had given away some of the information Samuel had revealed to her just this night. How was she going to talk her way out of this one?

"Margret, your mother and I have been aware for some time that you have not been yourself. You have been late to meals, withdrawn, and not as interested in spending time with the family as you once were. We know something has changed, and I believe it is time you tell me what that is."

Papa led her to the bench near the kitchen door, and they both sat. Although she wanted to respond to her father with another carefully constructed story that would appease him, the look on his face told her she needed to stop being evasive. She clasped her hands in the folds of her petticoats and looked away from Papa's knowing gaze. She would have a much easier time with the confession if she didn't have to look at him.

"Papa, you are aware of my friendship with a young man by the name of Samuel Lowe."

"Yes."

"We met three years ago when you were attending the secret meeting at the print shop before we sent our delegates to Philadelphia. Since that time, we have had several encounters, and he has kept me informed about the role he has played within his British regiment."

"British? Margret, are you telling me you have been keeping company with a British soldier for the past three years?"

"No, Papa." She paused and bit her lower lip. "At least, not exactly."

"Margret, either he is a British soldier or he is not." Papa reached out and took hold of her chin, forcing her to look at him. "Now, which is it?"

She swallowed, not wanting to say what she was about to tell Papa but knowing she had no choice. Licking her lips, she gathered her courage. Papa released her chin, and with a deep breath, she replied.

"He has attained the rank of lieutenant among the British, Papa, but he has spent most of his time coming to the aid of the Colonial army," she rushed to add.

"It does not concern me what else he has done with his time. What is important is that he has served in the British army and been a part of the men who have waged war on these colonies, overtaxed them, and made life here almost unbearable before we rallied against them and declared our independence." Papa stood and paced in front of her. His anger seemed to burn from every part of him. "Margret, I will not begin to list the dangers of associating with men like this Mr. Lowe. I will also refrain from expressing my disappointment that you would continue this behavior for so long without speaking with either your mother or me."

Margret had known Papa would be upset, but she hadn't expected him to be this angry. After all, hadn't she given important information to him regarding the British campaign?

"I regret what I must now say to you, but it is necessary."

She worried the folds of her skirts as she waited for Papa's next words, praying they wouldn't be what she thought.

"Margret, you are still unmarried, and I remain the authority where you are concerned. I tell you now that you are no longer to have any association with Mr. Lowe."

"But Papa—"

"Do not protest, Margret. You have been dishonest for quite some time, and you have acted in direct opposition to what your mother and I have raised you to believe. We do not have the liberty to take the kind of risks you have been taking of late. Despite the aid Mr. Lowe has given, the fact remains that he has still served the British as a soldier, and as such, he cannot be trusted."

Margret could hardly believe what she was hearing. The possibility of this command from her father had crossed her mind, but she didn't believe he would actually go through with it. She wanted to tell him that Samuel was the spy who had provided the information in August about General

Howe, but it wasn't her place to say. Samuel had promised tonight that he would try to see her again, but her every move would no doubt be watched. And she probably would not be permitted time alone outside anymore. How was she going to get around this?

"Now, I would like your word that you will abide by my wishes, knowing that I make them because I love you and do not wish you to be hurt."

She would have protested and assured him that Mr. Lowe would never hurt her, but Papa was in no frame of mind to receive anything like that from her. Seeing no other choice but to agree, she lowered her head and nodded. "I promise."

"Very well." Papa drew near again and offered his hand to help her from the bench. "Let us retire for the night. It has been a long day, and I fear the worst is not yet behind us."

thirteen

One week later, Margret learned that Thomas McKean had been appointed temporary president of Delaware in John McKinly's absence. The British had indeed moved forward and occupied Philadelphia, and with their continued close proximity, the legislature in New Castle voted unanimously to move the capital to Dover. It was more centrally located but also far enough away to protect the remaining important documents and provide the assembly a place to gather without fear of being overtaken by the British.

True to her promise, Margret remained obedient, all but giving up hope of Samuel's appearance. Once in a while, she would catch herself looking out the window and hoping she would see him riding up to the house. But she cast those notions off as fanciful dreams. Then she remembered what he had said about never giving up hope.

Papa had told her she could not sneak out to meet him, but he hadn't said anything about writing a note to him.

As September faded into October, the British pressed on toward Germantown. The farther away they moved, the more distance Margret felt between herself and Samuel. She had sent the letter to him by way of a servant, praying he wouldn't betray her. But weeks passed, and nothing. She had tried on several occasions to speak with Papa about Samuel, but he was always too busy to listen and preoccupied with restoring his shipbuilding business once the British left Wilmington and headed farther north.

With each passing day, she despaired of seeing Samuel again.

She didn't have any idea if he had attempted to see her or contact her, for she had been chaperoned at nearly every turn. Margret started to feel like a prisoner in her own home, and that made her want to see Samuel that much more.

The end of the harvest drew near, and with it, the time for their end-of-harvest celebration. This year, it was to take place at the Hanssen farm, and Margret was thrilled to have the chance to leave her home. . .even if it meant she'd still be under the watchful eye of her family.

"Do you not find this exciting?"

Her cousin Julianna spun in a circle, her hands raised high above her head. This used to be Margret's favorite time of year as well, but this year, her heart simply wasn't in it.

"Yes, it is at that," she said, her voice lacking any emotion.

Julianna stopped and turned on her.

"Margret. Talk to me."

Margret leaned against the wagon and shrugged. "What do you wish to discuss?"

"The reason for this state of despondence that seems to have overtaken the jovial cousin I once knew." Julianna joined her in using the wagon as a brace. "Where has the young woman gone who used to sneak down alleys or risk her life for an adventure?"

"I am afraid she is longer present."

"What happened?"

Margret summarized the events leading to Papa's edict. Julianna had been aware of Margret's continued association with Samuel, but she hadn't heard the latest.

"So once he learned that Mr. Lowe had served time in a British camp, he forbade you to have anything further to do with him?"

"Not only that, he has made certain I am never alone, fearing I might attempt to see Mr. Lowe when no one is watching."

Julianna nodded. "That explains why your father spoke with mine and asked that I stay close today."

Tears stung Margret's eyes at the hopelessness of it all. She had tried to reach Samuel with a letter but had heard nothing in return. She had tried to speak with her father, but he refused to listen. Now, during a time that should have been full of joy and celebration, Margret could only lament all that she had lost.

Mama approached from the Hanssen barn, carrying two large baskets with her. "Margret, Julianna? Could you lend your assistance with winnowing these dried beans?" She held up the two baskets and smiled. "It appears we have had a more substantial harvest than expected. That leaves us with far more to store than we had planned. If you both could help with this task, I can direct my energies elsewhere."

Julianna reached for one basket, and Margret stepped forward for the other. Mama held onto it briefly, causing Margret to look up. An expression of sympathy appeared in her eyes, and for a moment, Margret felt as if her mother might be on her side. During her forced confinement, she had had ample time to share her story with her mother. Mama reached out and caressed her cheek but said nothing more. With a sigh, her mother left almost as soon as she had appeared. Margret joined Julianna and set to work, throwing the beans into the air and letting the breeze blow away the chaff. At least she had something to keep her mind busy.

❧

Samuel crept behind the storehouse and peered around the corner to where he could see Margret and Julianna working apart from everyone. Would that he could mingle with them and approach undetected, but such was not the case. He had to put his army skills to good use.

"So, tell me more about your other encounters with this

dashing young soldier who has swept you off your feet with his charm and deception."

Julianna and Margret worked side by side, gathering dried beans and putting them into the baskets. The sun had begun to set, affording him the opportunity to sneak in between the many wagons scattered throughout the area where Margret's family worked.

Margret chuckled, and the sound was like music to his ears. He had received her letter but couldn't manage to get away until now.

"You remember that meeting by the willow tree, do you not?"

"I recall a handsome young man who seemed quite interested in more than mere friendship at the time."

Samuel grinned, in spite of himself. He felt guilty eavesdropping on the two young women, but he had to make certain no one lingered about before he made his presence known.

"And that interest increased as our relationship progressed... for both of us."

"Where do you believe your involvement stands now?"

Samuel pressed close to the other side of the wagon so as not to miss Margret's reply. Just a few more minutes, and he could talk to her.

"Honestly? I cannot know for certain. There were times when I felt it was headed in a certain direction, and others when it changed course."

"And the last time you saw him?"

Samuel heard the sound of dry beans joining the others that had gone before. The rhythmic pattern paralleled the cadence of Margret's voice.

"That was when I sensed he had much more to say, but the pressing need for him to return to his duties prevented him from doing so."

So, she *had* detected what he had been feeling, even though he thought he had been careful to keep it concealed. At least that would make his planned speech tonight easier for him to recite.

"And how do *you* feel?"

The work stopped, and Samuel held his breath, lest the sound of his breathing be detected.

"I have been miserable since Papa's edict, and I would give anything if I could see him one more time."

After a glance around to be certain his path was clear, Samuel crept to the back of the wagon and peered around the corner.

"Well, we cannot have you giving up anything for that, now can we?"

Julianna and Margret both turned their heads in search of him. Margret saw him first. He noticed the way she gripped the basket in her hands until her knuckles turned white. Her excitement barely stayed contained. Julianna merely regarded him in amusement and resumed her work.

After making sure no one approached, he crawled on his knees around the wagon and sat in front of Margret.

"I see that you are as happy to see me as I am to see you." He looked at Julianna. "Good evening, Miss Hanssen. It is good to see you again."

"Likewise, Mr. Lowe."

Just as during their other meetings, Julianna turned her attention to her task, allowing him and Margret a few moments together.

"Thank you for your note." He reached out and gently removed her hands from the basket, then he took Margret's hands in his. "I apologize that I was not more careful from the start."

"Oh, but you could not have—"

"Please, let me finish."

Margret appeared duly contrite and tucked her chin against her chest. Samuel freed one hand and tenderly lifted her chin so she was looking at him once more.

"My actions placed you in unnecessary danger more than once. In that regard, your father was correct in his concern. But it was never a lack of concern for you that led me to conduct myself the way I did. To the contrary, it was my strong regard and feelings for you that drove me forward."

Margret started chewing on her bottom lip, and Samuel smiled.

"You are no doubt aware that I cannot tarry here. It will not be long before another family member returns to collect your baskets, and I have something very important I need to discuss with you."

Worry formed lines in Margret's brow. "Please tell me you are not being given orders to leave again? I know the British have moved north from Philadelphia, but I do not know that I could bear it if you were to tell me you were once again leaving."

Samuel reached up to catch a lone tear that fell from her eye.

"No, that is not what I came to tell you."

He wanted to rush ahead and say everything he felt in his heart, but considering how her father felt about him, it would do no good. He must execute his plan with exact precision in order for it to work out the way he wanted. He only prayed that it would.

"Margret, my dear." He paused and watched as the realization that he had used her given name dawned on her. "You have been a light during my darkest times throughout this war. Whenever I needed a reason to keep going, I thought of you. I regret the errors in judgment which led to your father's distrust of me, but I am working even now to remedy that."

He could see that she wanted to say something, but she refrained. Instead, she allowed him the freedom to speak his mind without interruption, another facet that endeared her to him. He had reached the difficult part.

"When I leave here in just a moment, it will be with a promise that I shall return as soon as possible with the final part of my plan. And if all goes the way I pray it will, you will never again be forbidden to see me."

Anticipation and a smile lit her face, but she remained seated and controlled her emotions with admirable skill.

"Until that day comes, please accept this as my pledge to you." Samuel raised one hand to his lips, but instead of kissing the back, he turned her wrist and uncurled her fingers, placing a soft kiss at the center of her palm before closing her hand around it.

A gasp beside her made Samuel look over at Julianna. Tears gathered in her eyes at his gesture. He winked and returned his attention to Margret, whose eyes had darkened and whose hand tightened beneath his. She swallowed several times, her mouth working but no words coming out. Gathering every bit of strength he possessed, Samuel released her hand and leaned away. The sounds of voices drawing near spurred him into action.

"I shall return as soon as possible, my dear. Please trust me."

"I do," she whispered.

With that, he left the way he came, careful to avoid detection.

❧

Six weeks passed from that day that Margret would never forget. Although she had hoped Samuel's return would come sooner, somehow the waiting didn't seem so bad as it had before. Meanwhile, the British continued their advance, taking control of Fort Mifflin and forcing out the Colonial troops in late November. The victories achieved at Freeman's Farm and

Saratoga in New York, however, led the Marquis de Lafayette to believe that the patriots had a good chance of winning the war. He sent a recommendation to France that they lend their support on the side of the colonists against the British.

The tide seemed to be turning, and Margret looked forward to the day when reports of defeat after defeat of the British would arrive in town. The sooner that happened, the sooner she believed Samuel would be free to return.

General Washington took his men and retreated to Valley Forge for the winter, and Margret worked with Mama to prepare for Christmas. Decorations were set out, the food was prepared, and everyone's spirits had remarkably improved.

In the midst of everything, a knock sounded at the door.

Margret looked around the room where her family had gathered. Mama and Papa exchanged curious glances. Her brothers and sisters seemed surprised as well. Who would be knocking on their door on Christmas Day? When the knock sounded again, Papa stood and went to answer it.

"Jacob!"

Everyone heard Papa's exclamation and immediately moved from the parlor to the front hall. They crowded around the young man almost everyone had feared was lost to them forever, exchanging hugs and telling him how happy they were to see him.

One thing felt odd to Margret, though. Why had Jacob come to this house when he lived at the Hanssen farm? Movement behind Jacob caused Margret to peer over her cousin's shoulder. Her gasp when she saw who accompanied Jacob could be heard by everyone.

"Samuel!"

Papa immediately turned from Jacob and the family, his face showing his anger. Margret was about to rush to Samuel's defense, but he seemed quite capable of handling it himself.

"Mr. Scott, before you react and dismiss me from your home, please allow me to explain something."

Margret wasn't sure if it was the determination on Samuel's face or his tone of voice, but whatever it was, Papa nodded and allowed Samuel to enter. The family members quickly resumed their places in the parlor and sat in anticipation of what would take place.

Rather than take a seat, Samuel stood at the entryway of the parlor and looked at each person in turn. Margret watched him slowly look around the room. His gaze lingered on her but ultimately came to rest on Papa.

"I believe I owe all of you an apology for the deception I have practiced, and for the deliberate manner in which I involved Miss Scott."

Margret listened as his story unfolded and he shared every detail of their relationship, from the first meeting to the most recent. An overwhelming amount of love for Samuel poured from her heart, and she managed to tear her gaze away to look at Papa. Although he remained unmoving in his chair, she could see the effect Samuel's words were having on him. Silently praying that he would be receptive to Samuel's explanation and apology, Margret once again gazed upon the man who had captured her heart.

"As I have now been released from the majority of my duties, I have one final question to ask." He captured her gaze in his, and for a moment, time stood still. But then he again took time to give each person his undivided attention for a few brief seconds. "First, though, I must be assured that I have your forgiveness for whatever offense I might have committed against you."

Margret held her breath and looked at each one of her family members gathered around the room. Jacob had remained, and he nodded his head in affirmation without hesitation. Her youngest brothers and sisters also agreed. Nicholas took several moments before responding, but he finally nodded as well. That left only Mama and Papa. Margret managed to breathe as she waited for the final verdict, but as her heart pounded in her chest, she scooted to the edge of her seat.

Mama was the first to speak.

"I do not approve of your methods, but I cannot in good conscience deny you the forgiveness you seek when you had the courage to come here and ask for it. That alone is quite admirable."

Papa cleared his throat, and all eyes turned toward him. "Like my wife, I made it clear in the past that I did not find any merit in the deceitful conduct you insisted upon carrying out, especially when it involved my daughter."

Papa's face had started out stoic, but Margret saw his expression begin to soften. She closed her eyes and prayed, but not wanting to miss a moment, she opened her eyes again and silently prayed as she watched.

"Knowing what I now do about your methods and the underlying passion that drove you to make the choices that you did, I no longer believe you cannot be trusted. I am honored that you chose my daughter and saw in her what her mother and I have seen for years." Papa stood and extended his hand toward Samuel. "Thank you for being honest."

Samuel grasped the extended hand, and the two men shook hands in agreement. When the family started talking among themselves, Samuel cleared his throat, and silence again ensued.

"Now that we have that behind us, I believe I mentioned one more question I must ask."

Margret watched as Samuel's eyes sought hers and he bowed on one knee. Her heart jumped into her throat at what it appeared he was about to do.

"Miss Scott. . . Margret," he amended. "You no doubt are

aware of my feelings for you and the high regard I hold for your bravery, devotion, and commitment. More than that, you have come to mean a great deal to me, and I find that my life would not be complete without you in it. I do not wish for our relationship to stop at just friendship. I want it to last for years to come, and I want it to grow into a union that will be eternally blessed by both God and those you love." Samuel rested both hands on his one knee, his feelings shining clear in his eyes as he gazed at her. "With your father's permission, I would like to ask for your hand in marriage. I promise that I will treasure every moment with you and never again engage in deceptive plans. I want only to honor the good Lord and follow the path He shows me as the right one." He winked at her, and her breath caught. "Please, say you will marry me and make me happier than ever."

Margret looked from Mama to Papa and back to Mama again. Her mother smiled with tears in her eyes and nodded. Papa silently gave his approval, as well. Unable to contain her excitement, she rushed from the chair and threw her arms around Samuel, who caught her and prevented them both from tumbling to the floor.

"Yes! Yes! Of course I will." She hugged him tight. "Samuel, I love you."

He pulled her back and held her gaze with his. "And I love you, Margret."

Paying no heed to the family watching their every move and listening to the entire declaration, she tilted her head as he drew her closer and pressed his lips to hers to seal his promise with a kiss.

Never again would deception get in the way of the promises that had bound their hearts. Like her parents and her grand-parents before her, promises had sealed their fate, and promises would keep their family growing strong for years to come.

author's note

On June 14, 1777, in order to establish an official flag for the new nation, the Continental Congress passed the first Flag Act: "Resolved, That the flag of the United States be made of thirteen stripes, alternate red and white; that the union be thirteen stars, white in a blue field, representing a new Constellation." The first battle where this new flag was flown was the Battle of Cooch's Bridge in Delaware in September, 1777. Although not all sources cite this as the first battle, there is enough documentation from the Cooch's Library and the Delaware Historical Society to confirm it.

૨ઠ

The winter following this battle is the one Washington and his troops spent at Valley Forge, Pennsylvania; 1778 saw a turn of events for the better, and the Continental army experienced a string of victories.

૨ઠ

On February 22, 1779, Delaware signed the Articles of Confederation (the forerunner to the U.S. Constitution). But leaders from Delaware and other colonies were dissatisfied with the Articles. They urged the adoption of a stronger body of rules. John Dickinson and George Read of Delaware helped draft a constitution. On December 7, 1787, Delaware voted unanimously to approve the United States Constitution. It was the first state to do so, earning it its nickname of "The First State."

A Letter To Our Readers

Dear Reader:

In order that we might better contribute to your reading enjoyment, we would appreciate your taking a few minutes to respond to the following questions. We welcome your comments and read each form and letter we receive. When completed, please return to the following:

Fiction Editor
Heartsong Presents
PO Box 719
Uhrichsville, Ohio 44683

1. Did you enjoy reading *Deceptive Promises* by Amber Miller?
   ❏ Very much! I would like to see more books by this author!
   ❏ Moderately. I would have enjoyed it more if

   _____

   _____

   _____

2. Are you a member of **Heartsong Presents**? ❏ Yes ❏ No
   If no, where did you purchase this book? _____

   _____

3. How would you rate, on a scale from 1 (poor) to 5 (superior), the cover design? _____

4. On a scale from 1 (poor) to 10 (superior), please rate the following elements.

   ____ Heroine   ____ Plot
   ____ Hero   ____ Inspirational theme
   ____ Setting   ____ Secondary characters

5. These characters were special because? _____

_____

_____

6. How has this book inspired your life? _____

_____

_____

7. What settings would you like to see covered in future
   Heartsong Presents books? _____

_____

_____

8. What are some inspirational themes you would like to see
   treated in future books? _____

_____

_____

9. Would you be interested in reading other **Heartsong
   Presents** titles?   ❏ Yes   ❏ No

10. Please check your age range:
       ❏ Under 18   ❏ 18-24
       ❏ 25-34   ❏ 35-45
       ❏ 46-55   ❏ Over 55

Name _____

Occupation _____

Address _____

City, State, Zip _____

Presents

Great Inspirational Romance at a Great Price!

Heartsong Presents books are inspirational romances in
contemporary and historical settings, designed to give you an
enjoyable, spirit-lifting reading experience. You can choose
wonderfully written titles from some of today's best authors like
Wanda E. Brunstetter, Mary Connealy, Susan Page Davis,
Cathy Marie Hake, Joyce Livingston, and many others.

When ordering quantities less than twelve, above titles are $2.97 each.
Not all titles may be available at time of order.

HEARTSONG
PRESENTS

If you love Christian romance…

You'll love Heartsong Presents' inspiring and faith-filled romances by today's very best Christian authors…Wanda E. Brunstetter, Mary Connealy, Susan Page Davis, Cathy Marie Hake, and Joyce Livingston, to mention a few!

When you join Heartsong Presents, you'll enjoy four brand-new, mass market, 176-page books—two contemporary and two historical—that will build you up in your faith when you discover God's role in every relationship you read about!

Imagine…four new romances every four weeks—with men and women like you who long to meet the one God has chosen as the love of their lives…all for the low price of $10.99 postpaid.

To join, simply visit www.heartsong presents.com or complete the coupon below and mail it to the address provided.

$10.⁹⁹

Mass Market 176 Pages

✂ -

YES! Sign me up for Heart♥ng!

NEW MEMBERSHIPS WILL BE SHIPPED IMMEDIATELY!
Send no money now. We'll bill you only $10.99 postpaid with your first shipment of four books. Or for faster action, call 1-740-922-7280.

NAME _____

ADDRESS_____

CITY_____ STATE _____ ZIP _____

MAIL TO: HEARTSONG PRESENTS, P.O. Box 721, Uhrichsville, Ohio 44683
or sign up at WWW.HEARTSONGPRESENTS.COM